United States of Banana

Also by Giannina Braschi

Empire of Dreams
Yo-Yo Boing!

United States of Banana

Giannina Braschi

amazon crossing

Published by AmazonCrossing
P.O. Box 400818
Las Vegas, NV 89140

ISBN-13: 9781611090673
ISBN-10: 1611090679
Library of Conress Control Number: 2011904665

In memory and admiration of
Nilita Vientós Gastón & Chung Soon Fwhang.

Special thanks to Tess O'Dwyer, the Baltic Centre for Writers and Translators, Ledig House International Writers Residency, OMI International Arts Center, the New York Foundation for the Arts, Colgate University, and the City of Newark.

If Segismundo grieves,
Hamlet feels it.

Rubén Darío

Contents

Part One: Ground Zero

Death of the Businessman

It's the end of the world. I was excited by the whole situation. Well, if everybody is going to die, die hard, shit, but what do I know. Is this an atomic bomb—the end of the world—the end of the millennium? No more fear of being fired—for typos or tardiness—digressions or recessions—and what a way of being fired—bursting into flames—without two weeks' notice—and without six months of unemployment—and without sick leave, vacation, or comp time—without a word of what was to come—on a glorious morning—when nature ran indifferent to the course of man—there came a point when that sunny sky turned into a hellhole of a night—with papers, computers, windows, bricks, bodies falling, and people running and screaming.

I saw a torso falling—no legs—no head—just a torso. I am redundant because I can't believe what I saw. I saw a torso falling—no legs—no head—just a torso—tumbling in the air—dressed in a bright white shirt—the shirt of the businessman—tucked in—neatly—under the belt—snuggly fastened—holding up his pants that had no legs. He had hit a steel girder—and he was dead—dead for a ducat, dead—on the floor of Krispy Kreme—with powdered donuts for a head—fresh out of the oven—crispy and round—hot and tasty—and this businessman on the ground was clutching a briefcase in his hand—and on his finger, the wedding band. I suppose he thought his briefcase was his life—or his wife—or that both were one because the briefcase was as tight in hand as the wedding band.

I saw the wife of the businessman enter the shop of Stanley, the cobbler, with a pink ticket in hand. The wife had come to claim the shoes of the businessman. After all, they had found the feet, and she wanted to bury the feet with the shoes. There, I was talking to Stanley, the cobbler, because I too had left my shoes, a pair of pink boots, in Stanley's cobbler shop. He told me—you won't believe what I saw. I saw Charlie, the owner of Saint Charlie's Bar 'n Grill, watching the burial of the 20th century. Charlie goes out to hang the sign, closed for business, he looks up, and jet fuel burns and melts him down. And do you know how, how the torso hit the ground, how it landed. What I saw hitting the ground was a little bubble of blood, a splash that hardly felt itself, soundless, and dissolving into the cement, and melting without a sound.

I saw a passenger hanging on the edge of a bridge—with his feet in the air—his legs kicking—and both hands holding onto a steel girder hanging loose from the bridge—about to collapse—with the passenger—kicking his legs—as if he could peddle his way to the other side—where there is sand—sand and water—deep water—as if he could swim to shore and survive. The sand and the era of the camel are back. The era of the difficult. Now you have to climb sand dunes of brick and mortar. The streets are not flat, but full of barricades, tunnels, and caves, and you have to walk through the maze, and sometimes you'll get lost inside, finding no end—and no exit—and you'll fall into despair—but you'll see a dim beacon of light—appearing and disappearing—and when it fades away—your hope will fade—and you'll be amazed—because your pace will change. I used to be Dandy Rabbit, and now I am Tortuga China—not that I have lost my way—only my pace—because of the dead body I carry on my back—on the hump of the camel—in the desert storm—with no oasis in sight—but the smiling light of the promised land.

I saw the hand of man holding the hand of woman. They were running to escape the inferno—and just when the man thought he had saved the woman—a chunk of ceiling fell—and what he had in his hand—was just her hand—dismembered from her body. Now we no longer have the Renaissance concept of the Creation of Man—those two hands reaching out to each other on the Sistine Chapel—the hand of God and the hand of man—their fingers almost touching—in unity of body and soul. What we have here is a war—the war of matter and spirit. In the classical era, spirit was in harmony with matter. Matter used to condense spirit. What was unseen—the ghost of Hamlet's father—was seen—in the conscience of the king. The spirit was trapped in the matter of theater. The theater made the unseen, seen. In the Romantic era, spirit overwhelms matter. The glass of champagne can't contain the bubbles. But never in the history of humanity has spirit been at war with matter. And that is what we have today. The war of banks and religion. It's what I wrote in *Prayers of the Dawn*, that in New York City, banks tower over cathedrals. Banks are the temples of America. This is a holy war. Our economy is our religion. When I came back to midtown a week after the attack—I mourned—but not in a personal way—it was a cosmic mourning—something that I could not specify because I didn't know any of the dead. I felt grief without knowing its origin. Maybe it was the grief of being an immigrant and of not having roots. Not being able to participate in the whole affair as a family member but as a foreigner, as a stranger—estranged in myself and confused—I saw the windows of Bergdorf and Saks—what a theater of the unexpected—my mother would have cried—there were only black curtains, black drapes—showing the mourning of the stores—no mannequins, just veils—black veils. When the mannequins appeared again weeks later—none of them had blond hair. I don't know if it was because of the mourning rituals or whether the mannequins were afraid to be blond—targets of terrorists. Even they didn't want to look American. They were out of fashion after the Twin Towers fell. To the point that even though I had just dyed my hair blond because I was writing Hamlet and Hamlet is blond, I went back to my coiffeur immediately and told him—dye my hair black. It was a matter of life and death, why look like an American. When naturally I look like an Arab and walk like an Egyptian.

I was living on 50th Street in midtown—and moved downtown— two blocks south of the World Trade Center—six months before the attack—so that I could study up close, from the shore of Battery Park, the Statue of Liberty. I took ferries to the statue and bought books about the sculptor, Frederic Auguste Bartholdi, who on a trip in 1871 to Liberty Island, at that time called, Bedloe's Island, saw a stone fortress in the shape of an 11-pointed star—and realized—here on this 11-pointed star will be my statue. When I saw a cartoon of Bartholdi, in a children's book, drawing sketches for his sculpture, I was thinking that same fortress over which Bartholdi erected the Statue of Liberty will be the fortress where Segismundo will be imprisoned.

I was thinking: yes, he is on the verge of breaking out of the dungeon and all its chains. But I was also thinking—he should not be able to break out. Let's keep him inside to prove that liberty exists. A statue is just a statue. But to hear a man inside that statue—claiming he wants to become free—and never becoming free. We should charge to see him, but never free him. If he can't liberate himself—neither the crowd nor the police nor the firemen nor the army should liberate him. He has to do it himself. And if he grows old pushing the columns—and has no energy left to push, push, and push—and the media's attention deficit disorder turns the spotlight on someone else and the crowds forget all about him—too bad for him. There are enough problems in this city to worry about one man. And if he dies and the smell of his rotten body invades the city and brings diseases and plagues—will that be reason enough to split open the mausoleum of liberty? If an oracle says that unless we split open the statue—the body will continue plaguing the city—and there will be no peace—nobody will be able to sleep in peace.

It's not that we can't rescue him. We could if we wanted to, but we would lose a fortune. Segismundo thinks that he depends on liberty, but the truth be said—liberty has more need of him than he of the statue. The more he rattles his shackles and chains, the more tickets he sells. The military is afraid that some terrorist group will plot to rescue him. The people want to liberate him. Especially his own people—immigrants and prisoners from around the world. So, in order to prevent the coming insurrection, a voting system is created to give the people the impression that Segismundo's destiny is in their hands. They are given three options:

Wishy
Wishy-Washy
Washy

If they vote for Wishy—Segismundo will be liberated from the dungeon. If they vote for Wishy-Washy, the status quo will prevail. If they vote for Washy, he will be sentenced to death, and nobody will have the honor of hearing his songs rise from the gutters of the dungeon of liberty. Every four years the citizens of Liberty Island vote for Wishy-Washy. They can choose between mashed potato, french fries, or baked potato. But any way you serve it, it's all the same potato.

I read in the *Post* on August 11, 2001, about an attack by a suicide bomber on Jaffa Street, in Jerusalem, at Sbarro Pizzeria—and I was impressed by the mention of a little girl, 3 years old, who stood up among the rolling heads like Lazarus back from the dead, back to tell them all—*wake up*—and she saw her mother—sleeping beauty on the floor—and called her:

—*Mommy, wake up.*

The mother was dead. At this point a little piece of my glazed donut fell on the little girl's face and another crumb fell on her mother's legs. I picked up the pieces of my donut and ate them—the way I pass beggars in the streets—the worse they appear and the more they beg the more I ignore them, avoiding eye contact with the poor and thirsty—and as I turned the page—I saw the torso of a businessman whose testicles were blown off. He was screaming to a policeman who was passing by:

—*Please, help me! I don't want to die!*

When the policeman saw the man, he vomited on the stumps of the man's legs—and I felt the horror—but I ate my donut anyway, thinking:

—*I'm glad I'm not there. I'm here dunking my donut while others are blown to bits and pieces. Good luck. Keep hope alive.*

One month later I would be eating a glazed donut of the same kind when the first airplane hit the World Trade Center.

—*Tess! Tess! Where are you? Let's go!*

—I have to get my camera. And my pink ticket.
—For what?
—To pick up my shoes.
—Where?
—At Stanley's cobbler shop.
—Are you crazy! Let's run!
—No—Tess said—*I have to contemplate life from the highest point of view. That's what Emerson said it is to pray.*

So we went to the penthouse terrace—and from there we saw the second plane hit the second tower.

—They're going to fall!—I screamed.
—If they fall, they will fall on themselves—Tess said.

Bull's eye. What a prophet. I had told Tess when I was apartment hunting earlier that year:

—My only concern is the proximity of the towers. They will crush my building. If the Arabs came once to take them down—they will come back to finish the job. I know them. They were in Spain for eight centuries. They have a different way of measuring time. They are turtles. We are rabbits.
—But they were designed by the Japanese—Tess said. *If they fall, hari-kari, they will fall on themselves.*
—I don't want them to fall—I said.
—They won't fall—Tess said—*but if they fall, they will fall on themselves.*

So I signed the lease, on February 5, 2001, my birthday.

It is amazing, you know, when I was a kid we used to say, my friends and I:

—How old will we be when the new millennium comes?
—I will be 45, an old lady—I used to say—and by then I'll be dead.

But look at me now, running for my life, and wanting to go on forever and ever. Someday, I used to say to myself, I'll have my day in the sun. And it will be a happy day. A holiday. Someday, I used to say, I won't have to struggle to become because I will have come—come closer—every day to what I want to become. Oh, yes, that will be the day, I used to say, when I won't have to struggle anymore. I will be pleased with my achievements. And I want to achieve myself. Can that happen. I used to ask myself. It's not an enterprise, an ambition, or a goal I want to achieve—like a career—going from here to there—like running a race—where you sweat, you practice, and you get where you want to go. That isn't it. It was staring at myself—and looking at the sorrows of my changing face—and depicting the changes—and being startled when a new friend or foe appeared—inside myself—a new relationship between one state and another—from a face without a heart—to the sorrows of the changing face—to the painting of a sorrow. I always wanted to become myself walking the bridge across my past, present and future. Maybe, if I can remember smiling openly at the full moon and saying—I am round too. No sooner would my shape start changing—and with the sorrows of my changing face—new ravages, new debaucheries, new inequalities would force the smile off my face—as if happiness were everlasting and could shape other facets of my life. Take it easy—relax—don't worry—be happy. But foul weather came rushing through, and with age, other overpowering expressions signed their names around my eyes—as if they had never looked freshly at a fresh new day—as if spring could not stay green—because it had grown old and wrinkled—and a divorce between yesterday and today was becoming so obvious that the younger generation that was *I* was pushed over by another younger generation that called itself *me*—even when I insisted—I am spring. They would look at my forehead and say—no, you are not. If you don't spy on the mysteries of your changing moods, they become flat and sterile as if permanently in digression, looking back and wondering when it all happened. Can I stop it—at least for a second so I can have a chance to understand what is happening to me right now—at this exact moment. But no, what happens happens when it happens without excuses—it just happens that I was here—and I thought I would be here longer—while I was enjoying my lasting moods, the longer I lingered in the ones that I loved because they made me feel good and round—they would turn over—like a good dream that turns bad in the middle of the night—making me toss and turn until the position feels right—because I want to rid myself of strife—I want to have good dreams and a happy life.

I go to sleep at night and dream of teeth falling out and holes being drilled and filled with gold filling—and I see rain falling—wind blowing—cars running—fools thinking they are as smart as a fox—and the teeth keep hanging on like earrings on earlobes—and I feel my tooth is loose—it trembles like a bell—it will fall out—in a matter of time—I can tell—because I have good timing—and the pace it keeps hanging on is quite steady—so it is steadily feeling lousy and clumsy—but it is hanging on—it has a good sense of itself—it knows how to hang tough through tough times—like a soldier who, wounded by 20,000 slings and arrows of outrageous fortune, hangs on for life like my loose tooth that I feel trembling in my hand—like a newborn mouse—moving around and smelling my palm—so many metaphors to say what. I mean, what can I say that has not already been said 20,000 times.

I had tried to convince Tess to leave before but she insisted on going up to the penthouse. And when we came down to the lobby—I realized I had no shoes on. So, we went back to my apartment, got my shoes and my manuscripts, and came down again. To the lobby. By then the building was rumbling—smoke everywhere—dogs running—doormen crying—mothers with baby strollers. My neighbor passed me her dog. And the handyman broke open the first-aid cabinet and gave out masks. Outside it was snowing debris. We couldn't see where we were going. We ran toward the strobe lights of a patrol car—and knocked on the window:

—*How do we get to the other side?*
—*On a prayer.*
—*Which way do we go?*
—*Choose your own destiny.*

We headed south toward Clinton Castle, past the Chapel of Elizabeth Seton, the home of the first American saint and the birthplace of one of my masters whose bust is in the wall with the inscription:

—*Here was born Herman Melville, the author of Moby Dick.*

On the shores of Battery Park I saw a boat, and the captain was Charon sailing us through the waterways of Acheron—Tess was Virgil—and these were the waters that would lead us through hell. The captain announced the destination:

—*Liberty Island!*

12

At that moment, I held my neighbor's dog tight to my soul, reminding me of my own long-lost Scottie, Dulcinea—and looking back at the black clouds of Manhattan—the smell of Dulci's hair, greasy and soothing—I breathed deeply, that is where my inspiration comes from—from those white breasts—two breasts leaking—two towers falling—and the clouds keep hanging on—hanging on—and I feel the pressure of the hanging, that can hang me from a rope—tie me in knots—drive me into a toil—it is the hanging of expectation—of not knowing when or how—because I know not how it will fall, with fire, with choler, with water, or with death.

A La Vieille Russie

I saw a beautiful daguerreotype of a poet, in a shop window, dressed as a Harlequin. I am not sure if it was Baudelaire or Artaud. It had the eyes of Baudelaire and the nose and the mouth of Artaud. What are my masters doing in the window of A La Vieille Russie? I entered and to my surprise behind the counter was Vasily Vasilyich Gurevich, the owner of the most exquisite optik in New York, between Madison and Park Avenue, on 61st Street. From him I had acquired a collection of antique glasses from Russia, France, and China.

—Gurevich, what are you doing here? Business must be going well. Congratulations! Now you have two of the finest boutiques.
—Braschi, not really, I had to close my optik.
—Oh, no, my optik.
—The economy, Braschi. After September 11, I didn't sell a pair of glasses in three months. If it's not made in the USA, it doesn't move. How could I pay the rent? I had to close the business and get a job here. Look at this cabinet. I have these glasses that were from my optik. Try these on.
—No, what I love here is the installation. The theatrical experience. It's not only the glasses, it is where you hang them. From the eye socket of a skull, that is optik unique.
—Braschi, if I tell you it belonged to Sarah Bernhardt, would you believe it?
—The glasses?

—The skull. Look here, at the inscription on the back:
—*Squelette, qu'as-tu fait de l'âme.*

It was a gift from Victor Hugo to Sarah B[ernhardt ...] this skull as her prop in her legendary pr[...]

—You know, Vasily Vasilyich Gurevich, the British criticized Bernhardt because the skull was too white and clean—and it was not believable that this white skull could have been under the earth for more than 23 years. And she looked at the skull with adoration when she should have dropped it with disgust following the stage directions. What a mentality, I tell you! Of course she was fascinated. To see her future condensed in her past. Because the beauty of contemplating a skull—is that when you look at it—it is the moment when the past and the future unite in the present. Only in a skull do you see what you were and what you will be. I tell you, when my friends heard about the collapse—some of them smiled and wished me dead so they could relate more closely to the tragedy. I hate telling my story to these splinters who don't understand—and they don't care to understand—all they want is the scoop—and they're happy with the splinter and the splint. It's like misery loves company. Join the club of splinters and split your hair with a bobby pin. One of them said:
—Finally, the empire is falling. This is the beginning of the upset. What a defeat.
—Not because they fall will you rise. Why are you gloating?
—Because the fall will make other towers rise.
—Okay, okay. But the towers that will rise will not be the ones that laughed when our towers fell. It's not the laughter that rises. What rises is the curtain.

—What is a ruin?

—What remains as a thought—without a body—a ghost of dust and soot and debris.

—Would a skeleton be a ruin?

—Yes, but not a ghost.

—But why do ghosts appear in ruins? Why are their apparitions more certain when you have a skull in front of you? And even more disturbing.

—Because, I suppose, you have there the condensation of spirit and matter.

—Matter that is dead as a ducat, dead.

—Because both are ruins—and reminders of what was a memo, a syllabus, a footnote. If you tell me to choose between flesh and bone. I'm a dog. I take the bone because I have something to grasp. And figure out. Something to bury. And dig up again.

—And the body?

—You mean the flesh? Ah, well, you know the flesh flashes like teeth but doesn't have the durability. Phone books are cemeteries. That's why my number is unlisted. We are somber creatures with inclinations that twist us over edges as unpredictable as the flashback that is a ghost.

—Now, look at the floodlights.

—It looks like the projection on a movie screen.

—Look at the diversity of shadows—projections of ruins— reminding us: Keep hope alive! Keep digging! Maybe you'll find a hero in an air pocket where a bird laid an egg.

—Look at this twisted stump of petrified bone. A still life vanitas, a memento mori of what is left after we are all gone. See how, how a being after it is underground for more than eight years can still have hands and ribs and toes without a pound of flesh to cover the loins that are my bone marrow structure, my skeleton, my horse, my hobbyhorse. That's when the ghost comes in and drills into the skull all what inspiration is about.

—About what?

—Teeth—teeth that smile with little holes—pockets—air pockets—where a tongue can show its side—wet—to what avail.

—No purpose whatsoever.

—Except the liberation of thoughts.

—Hear the smoke of the ambulance. Ambulances always come with clouds of smoke. And then they disappear in a whistle. But what they bring is fear. Not freedom. Feardom is what they bring. And they bring fire and smoke. Oh, my nerves are bad tonight, yes, bad. I fear freedom. I, above all, fear the freedom that is above all feardom.

—This is too eerie for my ears to hear.

—Be placed at the ear of the conference like the dead body of Polonius that I carry on my back. And be happy. The worst remains behind this stump of luck. What do I see? Whose burial? Ophelia's? No, it can't be.

—It is a coffin. It looks like a pack of cigarettes. But it's a box of matches with nails inside. Who are they burying?

—The businessman.

—Who?

—The man who was petite. The man who was bourgeois. The man who was the center of the class, the class called petite bourgeoisie—the dealer of dirty deeds—dirty deeds exist to wash them out—and come clean—like my uncle always says with the smile of the villain on his face. And that is what I see behind these metal bars—the smile of the villain—the ghostly smile of the villain—and the Arab's greasy beard—that as a ghostly apparition is here inclined on the smile of the villain—emerging from a cloud of mushroom and fear.

—When those two towers fell—I felt a dentist had pulled out my two front teeth. I could not laugh anymore. And I have the smile of a smiling damned villain. But I also felt the hole in my mouth became a garage, and entering that garage were terrorists in trucks full of explosives and French diplomats—to fuck us more with other nations—to run over our dead bodies.

—Bury the one—bury the other—bury the twins—Muslim and American—Arab and Jew. Don't be unilateral. See the other's point of view. You are the whipper, cowboy. You whip and whip and whip—and attack, attack, and attack. Don't you know how to cover your ass? The attacker is never prepared to cover his ass. And to be fucked up the ass. But you will be fucked up the ass because you have fucked up the others too many times. Nobody knows you better than the one that you abuse. And I can talk. I know you well.

—You thought legs are not important—but now that liberty has no legs—it can't walk. And you thought legs mean labor— and you can find cheap labor in Mexico and in China. So you broke Lady Liberty's legs off—looking for cheap labor—and you found terrorists with explosives. You went for cheap—forgetting that cheapness is cutting liberty off at the knees. Now we cannot walk. What do you want us to do? Find cheap legs in other countries that will walk for us? You always thought if they want to walk—it's because they're poor. We go by cars and jets. But you forgot that fuel is a luxury and that it would end. Oil is coming to an end—and now we have no legs to walk.

—I thought the brain could rule over the legs. And I thought the brain was white and the legs were yellow or brown. And I thought I could rule with my brain—and even if I cut my legs off—I would find cheap legs in other parts of the world. But now I am a mutilated body. I lost my legs in Korea. I lost my arms in Vietnam. I lost my head in Kuwait. I lost my torso in the World Trade Center.

Piggybank

You think my brain is a piggybank. The only thing you do is throw some coins inside the piggybank of my brain. I hear the coins drop, drop, drop—but there is no water—they drown the stage in tears seven times salt. Even for an eggshell. My brain is a piggybank. Drop your coins and feel happy because you're contributing to my economy. Fundraiser, you are raising funds to kill my soul every day a little more. And when I tell you how I feel because all I have left are my feelings, you say:

—Good for you! You still have feelings! How fortunate you are to be capable of feeling!

But the question is:

—What am I feeling?

I am feeling cold hard cash falling flat like damp weather, like something cold when I crave something hot. It is always a disappointment to expect sun or vegetation and receive damp coins dropping—cent by cent—through the ceiling—as if they were drops of water. But there is no irrigation—only swarms of cockroaches—patches of mold—and holes being filled with senseless cents. It's like this—you are in your house expecting a furniture delivery or a TV set and a penny falls on your head.

—*Use it as you please.*
—*What will it get me? It can't buy me love or beef.*
—*Deposit it in the bank.*
—*In whose name?*
—*Mine, of course. You don't have a name because you don't have capital. You are living here by the grace of those coins that I deposit in your head every day.*
—*I don't need your pocket change. I need ideas.*
—*Ideas come with change. Ingratiate yourself with reality. You're in debt. You owe me your life. I am making you rich. You don't know how lucky you are.*

I wish I knew. I can hardly breathe but copper and nickel—and every day I eat the same chocolate coins at Starbucks, Kinko's, Staples. What a snoring age is this. I could make a Xerox in Starbucks coffee shop—and go for a coffee in Kinko's copy shop—it's all copycat commerce—the sameness is for sale—for bargaining—for usury—for the yawning of American poetry. Inspiration is the energy that breezes forward. The wish that keeps hope alive. Yawning draws backward. Déjà vu. Feardom. Not Freedom. Keep hope alive. Keep clicking. Maybe you'll click your way to the core of freedom. Click your mouse—click your remote control—and feel totally remote, distant, with an air conditioner blowing in your face. The marketers keep inventing desires, necessities for you and for me. I need this. I need that. I need. I need. It's the need of a smoking fit. If you don't smoke that cigarette now, you'll die—when in reality you die because you succumb to the rage and rattle of the needy greed that keeps you busy needing more and more things. Is this the American Dream—the greedy need—and the grim reality of the need that is never satisfied because it is red and tasty like candy—but it has no funds to support the greed. This is Chinese torture.

Copycat commerce.
Consumismo.

21

—I didn't bore a hole in your head. It was already there when I dropped the first red cent.

—But now it's really becoming a big hole—so big that the Twin Towers fell in it—and I hardly felt it—because I was so accustomed to the dropping of coins—that what difference does it make to have coins, or towers, or torsos, or pages of the *Daily News*, or tremors, or rain.

—Be grateful.

—Gratitude is your business, fundraiser. What am I supposed to do with 1¢, 20¢, 50¢ at the end of the day? I can hardly pay for my coffee cake. And by the logic of the absurd, you insist and actually believe that you're making me rich because you keep shaking my piggybank and counting the same coins over and over again. And besides, there were foreign coins in there that counted for nothing. They were immigrants like me. I immigrated with another speech, with another currency, to this economy where so many piggies are so happy being piggies that all they really want is to become cash machines—turning coins into dollars—and when you mention the almighty dollar:

—*Oh, my God*—they squeal with excitement—
dollars—dollars—mine—mine—mine!

But dollars, in my opinion, are too mute. I don't hear them singing and dancing like jingle bells. And sound to me is very important because when coins drop I hear them dropping—but dollars are too bland—made of paper—washed-out green—the color of envy.

What is your obsession with brushing your teeth—and flossing your gums? Every time I knock on your door you are cleaning your teeth—and showing them to me as if I wanted to see them. I don't want to see your teeth. It's as if you're saying:

—*Look at my teeth. They are as white as snow-white. And yours are yellow. Mine are sparkling clean. Spotless. Yes ma'am. I am a yes-man. I obey. I polish my shoes until they are squeaky clean— until there is no shadow of a doubt—on my teeth or my feet. I bathe twice a day so they don't smell. I have no smell.*
—*Open your mouthtrap, wider. Bite my finger and I'll scream: Ouch!*

Your smile is cheesy like your thoughts. It stinks of nothingness—of empty vacuum cleaners—of dirty dishes soaking in sudsy water—of nightmares—of dilettantes.

—*Cleanliness is next to godliness because the godly don't stink. They hide the evidence better. Their files are in order—behind their teeth. There is no evidence of dirty deeds. The files are missing from their teeth.*

I hate cleanliness because it reminds me of denial. You like to wash away the evidence. But I like things that are evident. I like what is seen *as is*. And sparkling, white teeth are not what they seem. When a mouth has been eating cheese, it should smell of cheese. I should be able to see the cheese between its teeth. I don't like to hide the evidence in order to come clean. If I were clean I would not have to come clean. I would just come clean *as is*—with my yellow teeth smelling of what I've just eaten. How will you know what I am like—if I don't show you what I like or what I am because I'm always brushing and flossing so my teeth don't stink of the cheese I've been eating all these years—and you don't even know that I like cheese—because I don't let you know what I like or what I don't. I don't like people when they pull out their teeth and wear dentures. When they talk, they slur like drunkards. I like drunkards when they slur the monotony of time as their teeth rot inside their skulls. What I like of skulls is that they have teeth—rotten teeth—and that they stink. Look. I need to know how you stink so that I'll know if your mortality matches mine. Open your mouth, wider, so that I can see the rotten mouthtrap inside— the mice running around backstage—the prompters—mouthing the script—the extras working as spies—the newspaperman with the scandal of the day—coming from behind the scene—like a bandit— to break the composure of those white teeth that are trembling when they break the news on their lips—and that work like moles—and that stink—because they show that their shadow of a doubt is falling out like false teeth. And so what if they stink. I have nothing against the smell of rot but something against what hides the smell of something rotten in the United States of America.

Smoker & Spender

I was a smoker and a spender. And I miss it. I miss my three packs of cigarettes a day and my shopping sprees through Bendel, Bergdorf, and Saks. I flew through those stores on a snort of cocaine—on a sniff of a roar of the bull of Broadway—charging expenditures that sounded like splenditures—splendid hours spent in shopping sprees—eyeing and buying the reverence of objects that bowed to me in silence. With each new sofa to fuck on, a new lover to fuck with, to feel young and fresh and sassy, to fill the hole of experience—and to feel new every day. As I get old, I get new. I'm a collector of *la buona fortuna, la buona vita*. Spending time, spending money—buying good taste on sale—buying prestige at full price—and buying power at all costs—to keep the eyes of the world on my extravaganzas—avoiding eye contact with the poor and thirsty. I have my own hunger and desires that keep flaring up like red neon lights. And how do I fill the hole in my stomach when I have the urge to buy and I have no money to pay my credit cards. Like a repentant sinner who won't repent, I'll spend more money and time shopping for the new and sassy—distracting the mind—consuming the time. The sweater. The skirt. The shirt. The gloves. The hats. The events to come where I'll play a role without a character inside—just the jingle of pennies inside my piggybank. I have claimed bankruptcy 20,000 times. Each time with more conviction—less guilt—and less shame. I claim bankruptcy and stash my loot in Puerto Rico—at my mother's house—all my possessions are safe there. I claim I have no money—and my claim is just and right—I am doing the right thing

25

for my soul—my soul needs leisure—my soul needs rocking chairs—caresses—my soul needs childhood—the red slippers and plush pajamas that make me believe in Santa Claus—so I claim bankruptcy. I need objective correlatives of leisure to fulfill my duty as an intriguer of the imagination.

I am unreliable—is that what you are trying to get at? Nobody relies on me financially speaking. But my shoulders are broad and open when it comes to a problem. Think of me as a dog. Why are you asking me if someone depends on me? Would you ask that question to a dog? When you come home from work I wag my tail and give you my paw and say:

> —*How are you? How was your day? Did they fire you yet? Do we have to move? Who insulted you this time? I'm hungry. I've been locked up all day.*
> —*Why haven't you eaten?*
> —*Because you didn't leave me any food.*

You walk in the door like a chicken with the head cut off. You don't know what you're doing. You might know what you're doing. Of course you know what you're doing. You're walking. What you don't know is where you're going. But at least you're walking. As the head of the chicken with the head cut off I can't walk. I am lying on the floor—half dead—watching you walk like a chicken with its head cut off. I want to lend you my eyes—so you can know where you're going—but now we are two separate entities. You can walk with your head cut off—and I can watch you walking—but I can't tell you where you should go. And I was used to being your boss. But you never wanted to be bossed around. And now I'm dying because I have nobody to boss around. And to think that I never knew I was bossing anybody around because I did it as part of my whole being. But you resented my bossing. You feel liberated without my head. And now that you have no head of state you brag:

—*The head means nothing. I am much more important than you. You can't walk. I can walk without you. I can still work without you. I just can't think or squawk without you.*

There's a mole here and there's a rat. The mole works in the basement and the rat works in the attic. I work in between. The mole and the rat are married. The mole informs the rat and the rat informs the boss of everything that happens at work at 5:00 p.m. sharp when the boss sends a limousine to take the mole and the rat back to Brooklyn. On their way home, they call the boss to inform him of every move I make during the day. Their job is to create instability on all floors except the basement and the attic because that is where they work. They keep the pressure on me—and I keep dreaming of tarantulas biting my feet—blood spilling and teeth falling. What am I supposed to do?

—*Look for another job.*
—*The market is shaky.*
—*You have no time to complain. Run for your life.*

I saw a head rolling. With no news of what was to happen. Just like that. In front of the entire staff. They didn't give any warning that the head would roll. The head just rolled, and blood was spilt. And the head that had cut other heads had to wonder: was this karmic payback for the heads I cut? Some rejoiced. Others were sad. Ding-dong. The wicked witch is dead! Who will be the next? Head honchos. Prepare your résumés. Your head will be next.

—I am a headhunter. I hunt heads for another institution.
—And do you think I want to work for another institution?
—Stay there and they'll slit your throat.
—I know they want my head.
—On a platter. But I've come to save your neck.
—You save my head from one guillotine. But you serve my head
up to another guillotine.

This is a vicious circle. This is the fishmarket. This is working for survival. This is survival of the fastest. This is the Darwinist capital of the capitalist world. A head afraid is a head haunted. A head haunted is a headhunted. Run for your life. Run from the guillotine to a head-hunter who saves your head and raises your salary—so you'll be caught in the red of the fishmarket buying gadgets to distract your fragile imagination that is cut in the red market of blood—running and escaping—running again—changing your résumé to update the fear you feel of being unemployed tomorrow—in the streets—and from there to welfare—and from there to begging. You're so abused by your boss that you have no time to think about the government. And that's exactly what the government wants—because the government does to other countries what your boss does to you at work. The government of this country is the boss of other countries—and it treats other countries like employees with deadlines. Obey your boss—you have an assignment—it is your responsibility to comply with the deadline—otherwise—we'll cut your head off or bomb the hell out of your country. No government or employee should last long—especially if you are a dissident or unless you are a dictator—then you can last long—because then you can be a boss—and do what bosses do—decapitate heads in the name of the freedom of the free markets. It's bureaucracy terrorism—not different from the other terrorism that marches rampant in the streets—oh, bureaucracy terrorists name the other terrorists cowards, but what are they—sinister cowards—because they cripple your resources. They take away your office, your computer, and your friends.

You're always struggling with the powers that be. You don't want power above you nor below you, and yet you obey out of fear of disappointing them. You're a stabilizing presence. They depend on your need to please—on your rage to prove them wrong. And yet, I don't see you as a destroyer of the power structure. You want to be what your boss is.

—*I want to be where he is, not what he is: an abuser.*

But when you're in his position—to abuse—you should abuse—because that's why they put you in that position. You turn your back on the powers that put you in power. Even the abused become confused and ask themselves:

—*Where is the boss?*

They were so used to the abuse that they miss the boss that you are not—and they resent you more than they resent the abuser. Their anger against the oppressor was energizing them, and you left them without an enemy—without a struggle to overcome—and still with a lousy job to be done—and no desire to do it. They want to feel the perils of evil—that not everything is peachy keen—that life is wicked. By cleaning up the act—you take out of them a big part of themselves—and they don't like it. That's why they chatter behind your back—that you're worse than a boss—because they don't fear you—and that's why they don't respect your guts.

And then, after you are fired, you can spend your life fighting the system, which will get you nowhere. Unemployment, degradation of the soul, one step lower than before, but higher in spirituality because you will identify with the guy you and your boss called with laughter a loser. And you'll exclaim:

—*That guy is me, arrogant bastard!*

And you'll realize that in that workplace, where you were a winner who laughed at the losers who did the job of the winners, none of them were your friends. Once you are out of work, you're out of friends. Unless you win the lottery. Nobody can save you this time. Why bother filing a grievance that grays your hair, wastes your batteries, and dumps your body into the garbage can.

What is long overdue in this country—and it's accepted that it misses its deadline—and never accomplishes its duty—and the bosses and the government—working in cahoots—say—*bravo! bravo!*—when it never arrives, and it continues failing to comply with the deadline. Long overdue is a revolution—a revolution against bosses who control your food, your allowance, and your nightmares. It would be so easy to step into one of those executive conference rooms—at the end of the long hallway where the corner office overlooks the Verrazano Bridge—and gun down the corporate board of directors—just shoot them in the head—it would be a crime for humanity and a cry for justice.

I have realized, living in this country, that in this country human beings display their arrogance, their might, their insomnia, their preoccupations, their ambitions, their fears—in the workplace—the war zone—the terrorist target—where bosses have loaded guns. Who better to personify the country than a serial killer—the Psycho Sniper in Washington who shoots random people dead in their tracks and demands a ransom in order for the bloodshed to stop. This nation, as the big boss of other nations, acts in the same way. It guns down other nations in the name of money markets. This is a serial killer nation. A nation of killers. Of bosses—not of philosophers, not of poets. This is a country of abusers and abused, of exploiters and exploited—and in between there is no music, no love, no beauty. The beauty is found in the decapitation, in the horror, in the bloodmass, bloodbath. This country likes the smell of blood—and it's attracted to blood like bloodhounds sniffing for dead bodies—and it doesn't know its limits—it stretches its limits to more dangerous limits until the killer becomes a suicide bomber. The killer in its urge for blood money kills himself when he finds no more blood or money to nourish his entrails. I say this with love in my entrails for a country where firemen were looking for survivors after 9/11/2001. My thoughts are survivors of this terrorist attack—they were found in an air pocket where a bird laid an egg.

White Parachutes

The suicide bomber is an explosion of a contradiction in its paradox, victim and victimizer, yin and yang, two sides of the coin, fire bomb and fire extinguisher, prosecutor and defendant, hangman and hanged. Heautontimoroumenos. A full cycle in himself. An orange, an apple, a world—round. Not part, but whole. To be one and the other, annihilating both. To be and not to be. Sed and Suida without the synthesis. No middle ground. No Wishy-Washy. One is Washy—the other Wishy—each affirming its being—neither integrating into the other. The water never quenching the thirst of the fire—the fire always wanting to be higher—never coming to terms with its own thirsty fire of desire—that means the time to hesitate is through—no time to wallow in the mire—try now we can only lose—and our love will be a funeral pyre—of the suicidal instinct—to repress one's emotions, to kill one's desires—to not be—and the desire to be more—not to hesitate, to go forward, to express oneself, to fan the flames of life—not to let go of one contradiction without exhausting the other contradiction. The bomber quenching his own thirst—the thirst for fire, for explosion, noise, attention—craves the media, the spectacle, the crowds. The suicider wants the final word, the Amen of silence after the explosion of fire, to extinguish himself in the funeral pyre. What the suicide bomber kills is the author of the crime, leaving the act behind. He can't be tried or fried in the electric chair because he kills the judge as he kills himself by judging himself guilty and condemning himself to death. When the killer kills himself there is nobody left to blame. Blame must always find a body. Somebody, anybody. So everybody starts looking around in suspicion of each other. Fuenteovejuna did it. The crime against society becomes the crime of society. So involved is the public that it no longer finds guilt in the other, but in itself. This guilt is the power of the suicider.

—Don't blame me. I don't exist anymore. You exist. You are the guilty ones. You should be blamed for their deaths. Not me. What did you do to me to make me capable of erasing all those inno-cent people—and myself—from the map of the earth?

The suicide bomber blows the anonymity of the crowd into indi-vidual pieces and pieces of individuals. Nobodies suddenly become somebodies with names, nationalities, stories, and faces. The indi-vidual rage of the crowd awakens when its collectivity is threatened. It's the fear that it could happen to you—or to me—or to any one of us—anytime—anywhere the crowd gathers. The crowd becomes an instant celebrity after being a nobody. The government worries that the roll call of the death toll will storm the polls and overturn elec-tions and cars, businesses and samenesses. When the government proclaims war against terrorism—it proclaims war against the awak-ening of the masses. What the suicide bomber kills is the passivity of the masses. Walter Benjamin noted the decline of the halo in Baude-laire—the decline of the sacred. But the halo of the poet is rising again. The halo of the poet rises when the crowd unites in one voice that becomes the voice of the individual claiming his voice through the crowd. The crowd says—*in my opinion*—and its opinion is always what it just heard—it is hearsay said here—by someone who steps out of line—to say—*in my opinion*—and a circle forms around him—a circle of the same opinion. And nobody else enters that circle, but the groupies. *You don't belong*—the groupies say. These groupies—I enjoy hearing what they have to say—these bunches of bananas or grapes—and I like their shapes—and how they fall out of favor at the height of their flavor.

It doesn't matter how often I hear: religion, religion, religion. I know deep in my heart that it is not about religion. It is about the battle of matter and spirit—the battle of the oppressed that are dispossessed—and want to possess—because they feel possessed. And they are possessed of spirit. It is the call of the oppressed to be possessed by something higher than material dispossession. After all the schisms of isms—after capitalism, socialism, Marxism, communism, feminism—after separation of church and state—it is an anachronism to call it a religious crusade when it is a global conflict between the ones who have too much and the ones who have too little, too little to lose.

Why do we count the number of dead as the relevance of a terrorist attack? The impact of the event should not be measured by the casualties, but by the possibilities it opens to other casualties, by the copycats, by the inspiration it produces, by the consequences of the act.

—*Only 3,000 dead*—I hear people say—*is nothing compared to the victims of AIDS or starvation in Africa or the earthquakes in Mexico or the tsunami in Japan.*

I don't count the casualties. I count the impact of the event on the collective psyche. Its relevance. Accustomed as we are to what is expected—war is expected—and casualties are expected. That is why the impact of the event cannot be measured by casualties—because that is what is expected—and impact is not measured by the expected, but by what has no name or tradition. It is based on the new. Success can be measured by numbers—and not just by the number of dead and wounded—but by the number of spectators around the world who witnessed the fall of the American Empire on TV. It changed the world's view of the self-proclaimed superpower. It made the superpower appear powerless. When success and impact come together, that event marks an era. There is a before and an after.

I used to worry about keeping my job, and losing my job, and what would I do without a job, and how would I survive without a salary, and whether to fight the system and sue. But now, as things are, I am more concerned about the Taliban than my boss. I am more concerned about my expatriate status than my unemployment status. Do I leave this country? Do I have enough money to survive abroad? And where would I go? Is Barcelona any safer than Berlin? I have two recurring nightmares since living at Ground Zero. One of white parachutes descending from the skies—invading us—ahead of our time—the avant-garde of warfare. The second is a white aerial vehicle hovering over Park Avenue—looping northbound, southbound— and after a few laps—everything around starts falling down—lampposts, traffic lights, awnings. If I have a third one, I will leave the country. Although, come to think about it, before I moved to Battery Park, I had another doomsday dream about an atomic bomb exploding over Radio City at Rockefeller Center. But that was not a white dream like the parachutes and the aerial vehicles. Those two worry me because I saw the white of fear in America's eyes. We don't fear the way we should fear. Our sense of danger should be at the height of our abuse. I get caught in bumper to bumper traffic jams of strangers—on curbs, in cabs, on bikes—I hear music from the back—and from the aisles—I have options—not this store but that one—and my choices are personal—my stops at shops, capricious. I turn around at the sound of a horn or a siren—or somebody speaking a foreign language that attracts me—and I applaud street performances. All distractions are welcome because they counter my thoughts. Sometimes it pains me to be alone—and I am surrounded by masses of people—alone in their heads—and the world is in turmoil. I don't know how to escape my silence. My mouth is shut—like a piano lid—or a store closed for business—until somebody next to me answers my thoughts. I don't know how my voice sounds—until I hear it—and it's not a matter of speaking, but of communicating. When I least expect it, I find the story I was looking for. I fell on the corner of 32nd Street and 8th Avenue. I tried to stop the fall with my hands, but even my control freak instincts couldn't stop my nose from breaking or my Gaultier glasses from shattering. I looked around to see what had caused my fall. A forklift had flipped me over onto my wrist, my knee, my nose. I was surrounded by construction workers shouting:

—*Put your head back!*
—*No, no, put your head down!*

Back or down, I couldn't stop from choking on the blood running out of my nose and my mouth.

Through the revolving doors came the head of security with a clipboard and a pen, and he handed me legal papers.

—*Sign here.*
—*Why? Why should I sign?*
—*Explain what happened.*

I was supposed to be catching a train to give a poetry reading at Bard College. Instead I heard the sirens of the ambulance coming toward me, and as the paramedics wheeled me away on a gurney, a black security guard came over and said:

—*You look bad, real bad*—and he rubbed two fingers together, saying—*your fall is worth money, baby, $100,000.*

All of a sudden, my brain turned from a piggybank into a cash machine. My eyes used to move as slowly as the eyes of the sages in Dante's Inferno, but now they had no time to reflect—only to count the cash that was spewing out of the cash machine. My eyeballs went blank before the cash was cashed. I have been writing poetry my whole life and receiving pennies for my thoughts—and feeling like shit—honestly. My worth is zero to the bone. The more poetry I write the more neglect I receive. People mistake priceless for worthless. But now I was cashing in. How much can I make on this accident. My nose was cracked to the bone. I had to get a nose job. The operation made my accident worth more. My lawyer who told me to have the operation—*so you can be worth more*—when he saw the new nose—said:

—*It looks worse than before. Go back to the surgeon and say that you need another operation. So you can be worth even more.*
—*Corruption*—I said—*cashing in on my nose. Twice. When you said it looked bad, I believed you. That's why I had the operation. To fix what was wrong. But I realize that what was wrong was your perception of me. You saw me as a cash machine.*

I don't know which was worse, my accident or my lawyer. For me, the lawyer—because he was cashing in on my pain and suffering. The first suffering was unavoidable. The second and the third, abuses at my expense.

Foreign Speaking English

I am writing in my foreign language, not in my native language. I am writing in the language that makes me grow into awesome thoughts. I encounter in my foreign language a culture that doesn't understand my native language. A culture that thinks I write from my stomach not from my brain because if I wrote from my brain—I would not be a piggybank—I would be a boss—a mandatary of guinea pigs—an office control freak—and I would not have to sweat like a pig—I would just plop myself in a big leather chair and drink coffee and speak through both sides of my mouth—but never mean what I say—never express awkward feelings. Feelings and smoking are strictly prohibited, but ass-kissing is highly recommended. Just say:

—Fabulous! Extraordinary! Sweet!

Never admit doubt. Never say it's unlikely.

—Yes sir, you'll have it on your desk first thing in the morning— even if I have to wipe my ass with a paper towel for dinner.

I don't mean to offend you, but good for me if you are offended. You show me your flag of pride—your Pledge of Allegiance to freedom of speech—but where is my freedom of speech—if I can't offend you—because you will recite a declaration of facts and notes of my impracticality, my insensitivity, my avoidance of the issue—to create waves—to imply that as a foreigner I don't understand because

I don't laugh at the jokes of the chattering mouthtrap of the smiling damned villain.

The problem with foreign speaking English, apart from it being flawed, is that it doesn't play by the same rules—it has its own passport—it could barbarize, it could terrorize—it could plant a bomb in the Oval Office—destroy national treasures—piss and shit on the roots of the White House lawn. Minorities will become majorities if we don't patrol the borders.

—*Howdy, amiga, bienvenida.*
—*Go back wherever the hell you came from.*
—*Shut the fuck up.*
—*Don't scream.*
—*Don't give excuses if you didn't do what you had to do.*
—*Don't tell me why you didn't do it.*

It is my desire to express my native self with my foreign tongue and to make my foreign tongue part of my native self. The fact is that speaking my foreign language I have become more distant. I hardly remember the tongue I first spoke—and as I grow and mutate in this language—day after day—I observe that some days I regress to the memory of the day I was born but my cradle is empty.

I have always looked for what is foreign to my nativity. I don't want to understand what I already know. I want to feel confused, be bewildered, sense awe, make the comfortable, uncomfortable. I want to misplace myself. When I am misplaced—I am noticed—as a misplacement—and I like to be figured out—as somebody who you have to keep misplacing, and changing the view you had, because the foreigner is invading the native—the native is becoming foreign—and in a country

39

where foreigners become natives—and natives foreigners—languages must be demolished and rebuilt—not on a geographical continent with a boundary called flag, but in the infinite space of a nutshell.

Familiarity doesn't bring nearness—it breeds stagnation—ease. Why am I drawn to what is hard to get, hard to achieve, hard to control, hard to center. The motion is always awkward and slow because in the process I lose control. What I do to control myself is shout and scream—the opposite of what is required of me to enter the grammatical system of my foreign language because in order to speak native with foreign I have to be who I am on both sides of the speeding highway—unable to cross—until I shout and scream my head off. Breaking the rules of the game means not playing by the rules of my native tongue or by the rules of my foreign tongue but by the rules of what is native and foreign to me—as a human being—in revolt.

We leave the revolt for another speaking term of four years maximum—at any location where tongues roll like dice—and there is no TV to program our minds, fabricate consent, steal elections, and change the subject with a remote control. Right now, we have to clear our objectives which are a little confusing, but such is the nature of the subject, as such, a controversial subject that needs years, to say the least, and time to organize parades of agitation, ribbons and flags. We don't need to create a slogan:

> —*All political parties are parted into piddley parts and partied out.*

When the economy falls over, we won't be jellyfish. We'll still have backbones and teeth, white teeth, and double standards to equalize the equilibrium that is never the same.

Tongue Machine

I'm in exile from the mother tongue—in exile from the foreign tongue—in exile from all the tongues that wag with the familiarity of knowing—with the credibility and the certainty—and without any kind of doubt that this is their town and country. I laugh out loud—and my laughter is as mother tongue as any laughter in any foreign tongue—but the joke is on me—because my laughter is not cheering for the other team which is roasting the barbaric tongue over an open flame of racist jokes and innuendoes—which is what the mother of all eggs laid in the foreign tongue wants—to leave me speechless—without a motherland—a land to mother my thoughts or a bed to lie down in. If I become a beggar in the streets, which is a possibility for an unemployed poet of underground revolutions, at least I'll know what to do when the abuser speaks native and I speak foreign.

Mother Tongue: *Get your feet off my sofa!*

Hamlet: *I beg your pardon?*

Foreign Tongue: *I am too farfetched. My language is foreign, Germanic, barbaric, but with you I am as native and intimate as a foreigner waiting for the master-slave relationship.*

Hamlet: *I never thought my mother tongue was my mother. I never felt the certainty of a mother tongue as the language of my house—of my fire—of my desire. I don't believe my mother tongue protects me from enemies. From what enemies have you protected me, may I ask? And now that I'm speaking in my foreign tongue—you—Mother—claim that you don't understand the language of my affections. The truth, Mother, is that you never understood my feelings. So, I became affectionate in my foreign tongue where I found a word named love to be chilly. You taught me the meaning of love. You said to me love means cold. So, I speak English—cold language of love—and my flesh shivers to the bone—brrrrr.*

Mother Tongue: *Hamlet, speak to me no more! Your words are daggers! Why do you torture me with English when my language is native? Why do I have to speak foreign to you?*

Hamlet: *I never thought lands belonged to languages. That a tongue controls a land, imposing its sovereignty, so there are no misunderstandings about the way we speak, our eating habits, our desires, when to laugh, what time to wake up, when to work, how to act at school, in a job interview, at a tennis match—and don't forget to wash your hands after you piss in a public bathroom.*

Mother Tongue: *Why were you such a fool to let them colonize you?*

Foreign Tongue: *I suck the blood of your economy, drain your natural resources, make you a beggar poorer in*

thanks—make you defenseless, powerless, home-
less, useless, speechless, foreign, more foreign, so
foreign that you'll lose touch with families and
familiarities so that you'll lose control of real-
ity so that you'll start hallucinating, wandering
with no return address, nowhere to go, bound-
less, without a chain to your collar, worse than
a house pet, a stray dog, in the air, like a bird,
spaceless and without wings to fly.

Hamlet: *When I spoke to you in my native tongue, you*
answered me with a wicked tongue—a tongue
unaffectionate—a tongue unloving and uncar-
ing. So, I decided to speak that chilly language
you taught me when you taught me the mean-
ing of love. I don't know if you understand me
anymore—or if you ever did. So now that I am
speaking in a foreign tongue I might become
more irrelevant to your affections. Who cares? I
am losing my speech in both native and foreign—
and speechless in native and foreign means with-
out a word to say—Ground Zero to the chilling
bones. Terrorized by both worlds that terrorized
me since I was born. And I lived with plenty of
illusions. First I said, well, if the native doesn't
like me, I'll become foreign to the native and
native to the foreigner. The foreigner will like me
because he'll see that I'm a monkey see, monkey
do. When in Rome I do as the Romans. And I did
like the monkeys. I climbed the monkey bars as
a foreigner becoming more intimate with natives

who had been foreigners in the first generation and who forgot where they came from and where they wanted to go. They were more confused than me because they didn't know who they were— even if they spoke native they were so foreign to themselves that they lost perspective—and I was always there as their mentor. But a colonizer never recognizes a monkey out of a jungle—and if this doesn't make sense—ask a colonizer of natives to make sense in his own language where nobody cares for him.

I am a foreign tourist. I have no roots. I am not a plant. I have a voice. I sing. I sing from my stomach and I sing from my brain and I sing from my diaphragm and from my womb. I rock in a cradle and I piss and shit on roots. I am not stuck in dirt like a plant. I walk on my feet and conduct with my hands an orchestra of thoughts. They all sing from different locations—from the balcony—from the basement— from the address where I left off yesterday—from the e-mail I don't know how to open—from a gift I opened last night (the package gave me anxiety when I opened it)—from nobody is home—home has no return address—no telephone—no TV—no e-mail—nothing that comforts my spirit—nothing that says I live here because I was born here because I don't believe my country is the place where I was born nor the one I was raised to be who I am and I don't have a *who I am* in *I am who I was* or *who I will be.*

Chicken with the Head Cut Off

There are two movements in the history of colonization: invasion and immigration. Emigration is a reaction to the invasion of a nation. Because they have been invaded—they will emigrate. This is about changing perspective from the point of view of the colonizer to the point of view of the colonized. The colonizer organizes the invasion but doesn't prepare for the counter-invasion. The colonized moves from the land of the invaded to the land of his invader with the same adventurous spirit of the conqueror—not to avenge with arms but to reap the spoils of war—to infiltrate that new culture and to conquer it with his own culture. Now, he is two. He speaks the language of the invader and the language of the invaded. His experience is bilingual. It is very hard to be two—and two who are in love—but their love doesn't match—it doesn't fit—it has larger legs than a giant—and a very short neck—or it could be an abomination—like the Royal Academy of Spain has declared Spanglish—but it is the language of the new man. The Renaissance had its man—Il Cortesano. The 20th century had its man—the businessman. The new man is a messenger. He is a mixture of races and cultures. He has Chinese eyes—blue or hazelnut. He has freckles and an afro. He speaks Spanglish with a Russian accent. Cold turkey leaves me cold. I will never be roasted on Thanksgiving Day—although I like the holiday—because it is a holiday just to say thank you. I like Pilgrims because they are on a pilgrimage—and they don't have to finish the unfinished business. Hamlet and Segismundo are princes of Denmark and Poland, but their native tongues are English and Spanish, so when I read them, I read them in exile—in exile from the language of their native land. This distance from the native makes me love more the foreign. Socrates prefers to die in his homeland than to live in exile. I prefer to live and never feel at ease in any land or language. I wonder why I was chosen, but I also wonder why the chosen are never the most prepared—and why they are chosen when they never asked to be chosen. I read Dante in Spanish and I read Dante in English, but I have never read Dante in Italian, *anche parlo italiano e sono italiana.* I'm more French than Beckett, Picasso, and Gertrude Stein. I hear the voices of Artaud, Rimbaud, Baudelaire, Montaigne, Rabelais, Villon, and Joan of Arc. They all want to write a part of my Hamlet and Segismundo. They all want to say something. And Artaud and Rimbaud are constantly fighting in my house—barking like dogs—and insulting each other. That they insult each other is kind of amusing—except when they involve me—blaming me for not being a good enough medium for their thoughts. If I'm not good enough—then get out of my house. Then they laugh the laugh of the Medusa—because I answer them—and that is what they want—an answer—constant attention. Baudelaire is more lax. Sometimes too indulgent. Always buying strange glasses and books to read—a collector of toys and antiques—a decadent. And always looking in the mirror, taking a peek at my face, and sizing up my hair and clothes, ready to criticize my underwear and my external affairs. Joyce thinks he is better than all of them and can only be compared to Dante, but Dante is already in paradise and doesn't want to talk to him or to anybody but Beatrice. Colonize your colonizers—they say—learn from those bloody bastards. Which bastards—I ask. The American bastards—they colonized your colonizers—Spain and England—and look how phony they look—like prairie dogs—following the Bushes into the oil fields of Iraq. With all these writers in my home, I hardly have time to write. They keep interrupting my writing. If I am listening to Joyce, Artaud storms into my brainstorm, interrupting Joyce who is hard to stop—but Beckett is happy—because they had a stormy marriage—they were upset that I turned out to be a girl and not a boy. They would have liked me to be named Dante not Giannina—so they could claim a lineage to the past. These fights drag on—and Joyce gets drunk—and Rimbaud wants sex—and Artaud wants to get out of the mental asylum—Baudelaire loves the masses and clothes too much—and Artaud loves suicide bombers and pulls Rimbaud's greasy hair and lashes his tongue at him. Why don't you two become lovers—but they hated their bodies—then become Muslims—but they hated the Jews too—and I was caught in the middle of the screaming match. *Soy boricua.* In spite of my family and in spite of my country, I'm writing the process of the Puerto Rican mind—taking it out of context—as a native and a foreigner—expressing it through Spanish, Spanglish, and English—*Independencia, Estado Libre Asociado*, and *Estadidad*—from the position of a nation, a colony, and a state—Wishy, Wishy-Washy, and Washy—not as one political party that is parted into piddley parts and partied out. Hamlet crawls between madness and suicide—like he crawls between loving Ophelia—and loving her not. His fantasies of madness and suicide become realities in her. She is the doer of his being, of his eternal doubt and vacillation. Hamlet would have never wanted to kill his father—because he loved being under his control—and even when he has no father—he still feels controlled by his ghost. He needs an author. Zarathustra talks of the Death of God—but he wants somebody to replace that God—the overman. I too need control from the top—not because I lack control—but because I lack authority. The author—I have never been. I'm a player—and I want to be played upon. I can't authorize. I don't like the way Hamlet deals with his father. Too much of a kiss-ass. I love that Segismundo wants to throw his father off the balcony for locking him up in the dungeon. I only wish Segismundo didn't forgive his father. Why? It is not forgivable. And it would be more radical as a Greek tragedy—as something that couldn't be undone—as an answer to the Oedipal complex—kill the father—consciously—not unconsciously—knowing that he deserved to die. And I would have liked Hamlet to beat Claudius at his own game and inherit the throne. Hamlet, the king. And I would have liked his relationship with Ophelia to be more on par with his relationship to Horatio. Let Ophelia recoil when Hamlet is about to reach orgasm—at that moment let him curse her with the gift of prophecy—so that only she can see and nobody will believe her. And then Hamlet would cut his ear off and send it to Ophelia in an envelope. His ear would be the prop of madness representing the critical mind of the modern artist who goes ballistic. Hamlet doesn't need to commit suicide, society does it for him, it fabricates proof against him when his madness is most lucid, right on target, right on cue, like Artaud and Van Gogh. T. S. Eliot says Hamlet has no objective correlative—but how can I have an objective correlative when I lost my job? The objective correlative is an absence I miss—a hole I want to fill with a character that breathes through my life every single day. I wake to this absent presence—that has no objective correlative except in what I want to exist—not in what exists. And even if I find a job the job would be what I do not what I am. So, again, the objective correlative would be in absentia with no sofa on which to rest my weary feet. Oh—people tell me—why are you so ungrateful to those who support you and so grateful to others who give you nothing. I am grateful when I find people who understand me and whom I understand. When these people enter my life—we are usually eating under the table—and doing illegal transactions—under the table—as illegal aliens who have to eat leftovers—scraps thrown to the dogs—and we chew those bones—and make collections of bones—and bury the collection of bones under the earth—only to dig them up again with

our paws—to rediscover trinkets, teeth, or shards—and they are treasures—new world treasures that musty and bored four-eyed scholars
will unbury one day—and exclaim: Eureka! *Yo-Yo Boing!* Inside this
treasure chest are languages in transitory states, minority verbs without a status quo or a nation, sounds of laughing children with baby
teeth ready to suck the milk from the udders of the motley cow. Bilin-
gualism is not the language of the fatherland or the motherland—but
of udderlands that are free of motherlands and fatherlands. Emi-
grants move their tails while they walk—and they bury their roots to
dig them up again—and eat them because that is what roots are for—
to be dug up and eaten by a stray dog howling at the infinite and
sinking in quicksand. And, while the dog becomes smaller and
smaller looking at the infinite migratory combinations that can drive
him crazy because there is no limit except the horizon of the Promised Land, *las vacas sagradas* keep chewing the same ol' cud and
never get tired of posing in public like the pope—and no matter how
old—they never abdicate their throne. But they abdicate their art
and become politicians ruled by visibility—ubiquity. They become
writers of the market—publishing the same book every few years—
using the same structure—plotting while yawning. Not even if they
cough a thought would they recognize the germs of a new beginning—and if they don't recognize themselves in themselves anymore—they look for the audience that was there the first time—
afraid of risking what they have—and so it is always more of the
same and nothing new. How do you not realize you're repeating
yourself? That your record is not just scratched—it's worn out. Your
bank account has a zero balance. You ran out of gas. You have to fill
your tanks. You have to withdraw from the panorama. You have to
learn how to be yourself again. The same, but in another encounter
with the same—it's not the same, but another who speaks to you and
recognizes you as different. Like when I walk and walk the same

streets over and over again—year after year—looking for something new when the new thing here is me—in myself—me in myself is new when I recognize my capacity for transformation. Metaphors are the beginning of the democratic system of envy. They look for what is dissimilar and try to make it similar. Everything that is similar cuts the edge of what is unique. Everything is related to something—and if that cutting edge can be cut shorter or rougher—better. The power of the poet is in his hair. His fertility is counting grains of sand like strands of hair. Pardon my lack of reference when I disjoin metaphors. Instead of making comparisons that work I make comparisons that don't work. Duchamp's bicycle is the modern metaphor because it is a useless comparison—it doesn't join—it disjoins—it tries to unite things that can't be united—and nevertheless the stool and the wheel that I can't ride like a bicycle creates music. I can elucidate its thought—shine on its shadows, blow on its horns, whistle the thought, chant the memory, and play the saxophone.

Writers have forgotten the subject matter. They think they can substitute matter with plot. But where is the subject matter? The subject matter that matters is the market value of the plot. What matters is triviality, banality. I am neither against banality nor against triviality. But I am not a scribbler. I like scribblers because they babble bubbles— and out of the bubble bath they come out clean and refreshed. But writers are stripped of the distinctions that exist in writing. Even the prizes are nondenominational. They are given to more of the same and nothing new. Old would be good if it tasted vintage—but it has no taste or odor—it is the odorless tastelessness of more of the same and nothing new. It runs in the family of no distinction—envy, democracy—of more of the same and nothing new. It will not turn me into a vegetable. It tries to serve me as a side dish—to pass me off as a carrot—but I am not orange. I am juicy like a steak—and I am the leader of that plate. I am a subject that is a head—not a complement of a chicken that has no head. The subject has become the passive observer—the spectator— waiting for the curtains to fall like the guillotine. Artaud said theater can exist without the text—the production has to liberate itself from literature—and it did liberate itself—it became self-sufficient—it became a conjugation. I was backing Artaud—cut the head—cut the literature, cut the text, cut the letters. Make it a verb—an action. What is not functional should not exist. Off with their heads. Revolution—cut the heads of states. Cut the poets, the philosophers, the minds. Now what do we have left? Politicians and preachers who conjugate the past— past orders of the past—and instead of great thinkers who cut the head of God a long time ago—now we have chickens with their heads cut off. Pirandello was right at his moment: *Six Characters in Search of an Author*. The author is dead. What are we going to do about it? Don't substitute God with author. Don't replace death with more death. I should not be thinking in a straitjacket of a sentence structure that is also dead. I am drunk—and I don't have a body to jubilate my drunkenness. My thoughts are stuck in my head—full of wine and cheese— memories and worries. My head needs an agitation of some sort—a revolt in the files—to produce flashbacks—to return the subject matter to the place of the subject matter—to alleviate my head. Verbs jump back into their places and die when they become what they were. They already were there—and once they start replacing each other—and recognizing that they can function in different places—without their traditional meaning—that meaning—real meaning is created out of a dissatisfaction with the past—a displacement from comfort—a refusal to sit tight. Originality is going back to the place where you were what you were—and finding an empty chair. Would you gladly sit on it? No, thank you. It is empty for a reason. That's where my ass was. Not where my head is now. Now that I am seated in the audience watching feathers flying, claws scratching, blood splattering, I should not be nostalgic, wishing I were there on stage—on top of that headless chicken—giving it meaning and unity. No, that would not be a happy ending for a chicken that is jumping for joy to be free of my commands—free of subjugations—and I believe in all kinds of liberation—and I will cheer that headless chicken until we both die of sheer jubilation.

Hurray! Hurray! What a great chicken! The president, the secretary of state, the businessman, the preacher, the vendor, the spies, the clients and managers—all walking around Wall Street like chickens with their heads cut off—rushing to escape bankruptcy—plotting to melt down the Statue of Liberty—to press more copper pennies—to breed more headless chickens—to put more feathers in their caps—medals, diplomas, stock certificates, honorary doctorates—eggs and eggs of headless chickens—multitaskers—system hackers—who never know where they're heading—northward, backward, eastward, forward, and never homeward—(where is home)—home is in the head—(but the head is cut off)—and the nest is full of banking forms and Easter eggs with coins inside. Beheaded chickens, how do you breed chickens with their heads cut off? By teaching them how to bankrupt creativity. By spending their energy declining verbs:

I do	*You do*	*We do*	*They do*
He does	*She does*	*It does*	

Everything is in the doing. What can I do for you? What can you do for me? Scratch my back, and I'll scratch yours. I can pilot a jet. I can order a salad. I can rollerblade. I can write a play. I can fall in love. And I can do what the subject matter could never do—decline verbs—and subjugate subject matters to become attributes, compliments—feathers in the cap of a chicken that walks like a chicken with its head cut off. Ask me if I can. But never ask me who I am. Because that can only be answered by a being. A doer cannot be. A doer can only do. I am what I do. And if you ask me: who are you? I'll blink my teary eyes and feel pity for my lack of being—and I'll threaten to kill myself, but I'll have no self to kill. I'm caught between two psychosomatic dilemmas—the one that wants to sleep at night in your fat lazy arms of comfort and the one that cheats on your fat lazy ass. Serves you right, old fart, for making me do what I don't like to do just to support you. Life is short but it feels so long. Serves you right that if I die you get nothing because you've spent it all. You didn't earn the respectability or the visibility or the bread and butter. Serves you right to get nothing—you earned it. I made it—you blew it. My wallet is empty like my life, misspent by my wife. And when I lost my head, I lost my statehood—where I could learn to decline other verbs:

—*what was*
—*what is not*
—*what does without knowing what was is not anymore what is*
—*and what I do has nothing to do with what I am.*

I was commanded by a subject matter that mattered—but now I am repeating ad nauseam the same conjugation because I killed the subject matter that matters.

I read	*I scream*	*I weep*
I do	*I jump*	*I kiss*
I play	*I pray*	*I fall*

I am, I am, I am—what I do when I do what I have to do. My being doesn't exist, but when I do, I bring my being into a state of forensic frenzy, and I do what I have to do always. I always fulfill my deadlines because they are the lines of death, and I can never skip what was meant to die by a deadline. And that is my goal. To die when I get to the deadline.

Language of Mass Destruction

This is the era of ticks and dust—of convents and seminaries—of nuns and priests—of clerics and sheiks—cloaked in black robes—the color of obscurantism. See no evil, speak no evil, hear no evil. Speak now or forever hold your peace. Eat now or forever hold your tongue. Bite your tongue if you don't speak now. I will speak tomorrow, even if I don't eat now. Nobody will hold my peace or send me to sleep. Nobody will substitute one reality with another reality. But realities are doomed to collide. One being devastated and harassed by the other. The other.

Identities are not tangible anymore. If you look for an identity you find inequality. If you look for similarities you separate one truth from another. The self has been refracting. Decimals are decimating. Solutions are not consulting consultants to find jobs. Jobs are out of work. Meaning has become so valuable, so huge—so stupendously absurd, so useless—such a glittering object of desire—it glistens—it supersizes all the shapes. The forms have shrunk. They are crouching in shame for having been consumed by the fads of consumerism. Now this immense prodigality—this giver of gifts—this creative energy in our muscles, bones, cavities, and caves of our brain with juices of jubilation and rage to transform, to not be deceived, conceited, alienated, defeated, minimized—drawn to a corner—surrounded by four walls—seated. This is what bothers me the most—why seated—why do we have to observe—laziness—and all this introspection is dying inside without an objective correlative.

We attack on false premises. We have nothing real to give and plenty to take. We take what you give, and if you don't give it willingly, we enforce our rule of law, democracy, and free trade agreements until you comply with the deadline. It is time to take the center and move it to the corner. We don't need the center. We need to strategize the margins. In the margins are the whistle-blowers and the asides.

The time is out of joint. Nothing fits because forms are empty of meaning. Preconceived notions of reality are coming down like the Twin Towers. Democracy is obsolete. It's an empty formula. A charade of rules and regulations. What we live is not what we say we are living. Our standards of expectations are not supplied with sufficient material. The right wing is the wrong wing. Correct is incorrect. The joint is out of joint. And the charade is over. Inequalities are survivors. When I multiply the loaves of bread and fish, the minuses are larger than the sum of the parts. The sum of the parts is always smaller, and it occupies a smaller place. What is small is mass-marketed as a big fish in a big pond. But the eye can see the lie is bigger than the fish and the pond. Just because something doesn't fit, it doesn't mean that it is a misfit, but that it has a possibility to be treated as a special case. The pack of lies has not changed size—but the lies don't fit the pack anymore—and the seamstress can't make it seamless anymore—the stitches are showing. And the charade is falling like a wig. And when hair falls out it's not necessarily a bad sign. It's a good omen that hair falls out—that kairòs is approaching—opportunity has no hair on its head—and the statements that come out of that head are as bald as a jagged-edged knife that cuts inhibitions loose of dogma—loose of strife—loose of hair—like a gap full of light.

People are not equal. Some cannot be considered part of those that add up and multiply races and specimens. Some are subtracted, others divided, but the majorities are birds of a feather that flock together. Not every pigeon is a rat with wings. Not every rat with wings is a dove of peace. The constitution of one wing is not the right of another thing. I have inalienable qualities, not rights. I have no inalienable rights, I never had them—so I developed my inalienable qualities. Rights are full of privileges—and permissions—and escape doors that don't allow everybody the same access. Everybody is not anybody, somebody is not nobody, nobody is not anybody. Whether these bodies have penises or vaginas—feathers or beaks—they can be bodies of anybody, somebody, or nobody. When nobody is home, somebody says: if nobody is home, there is nobody to answer the phone. I never saw what was inalienably right, but I always saw what was inalienably wrong. And I struggle to make ends meet, although they never meet at the end. The end never meets the beginning. They are in trouble. Both the end and the beginning don't find ends meet, and they don't match, they don't fit, they are unequal. I part and depart from a principle of inequality. Nothing is the same under this majestic roof of canopy. Some people think and some fly like rabbits—and others walk with their houses on their backs like turtles—but they are not turtles. I can't say that this is like that. Metaphors and similes are as lazy as the democratic system that creates all men as equal fools under the same canopy of generalities when they don't know how to form a particular thought. I said nothing—and I meant everything under this majestic roof of canopy—puppies and nuts—bounded in a nutshell. I believe we are born uneven. There is rarely a pair thought except from the mouths of clones or clowns like Rosencrantz and gentle Guildenstern and Guildenstern and gentle Rosencrantz. Why were they the same? Because I don't recall their thoughts—just that ambition is a shadow—and that my ambition was as shallow as a dream's play—or as a shadow's shadow which is a metaphor or a simile or another worthless pair that isn't inclined like a pear to find an angle or change its shape. What comes out of a womb is uneven and terrifyingly beautiful. I added the compliment of making it beautiful—but terrifying complements the compliment and completes the uneven thought—and doesn't take an iota from the idea that it can be round which means full—and fullness is always uneven—it's always heavier at an angle—and life never gets even with itself—even with all the grudges I've had to avenge—I never got even with myself—because I never confronted myself in the mirror of myself. I should have gotten even with myself—but I avoided myself until the last syllable of silence—when memories got even with my present—and kept me from living in the moment. They are so unjust and uneven and unpredictable—those memories. I can't get over the injustice. Justice is a fallacy of inequality, and power reaffirms itself through instances of inequality. Watch for those daily struggles of inequality. Thirst is uneven—and smell smells better when it is uneven. Noses are particular but more uneven than 11—but who needs a formula to prove the unevenness of life—when a maggot can claim a portion of a fig—and even if the fig is complete in itself—like a grape—it can be eaten alive—by cannibals—and who says we are not cannibals. My principle of inequality sees an eagle and flies like a lamb—but I am no ham—although I like to eat them. I am no eagle. I am a rotten egg. No, I was a chicken when I laid eggs. Now I am a man—with no principle at hand—but the principle of inequality, which means every time I try to match a pair of socks I find that they stink. Equality is always holding grudges against inequality. But all inequality really wants is to get even with equality—by making equality uneven—and giving it the finger:

—*Fuck you! Keep your job! Keep your stripes! I want my independentista life.*

I am going to start my own business. I am going out on my own. But then I look at my bank account and see zero to the bone. I can't quit. Not yet, anyway. I look at myself in a mirror. I see I am getting old, but I lack advancement. I was supposed to be my own boss by now—because I am a good boss—and my bosses know it—that is why they are always checking on me, keeping me down, clocking my hours. Was I out late last night because I was late again this morning, and I'm disheveled and distressed—and I don't know what to do. What should I do—take a gun and shoot myself—or pop some sleeping pills—to dream, perhaps to sleep—ah, there's the rub. Why would I give them the benefit of the doubt? Why prove them right?

—*You see. What a complicated person, a troublemaker. Always on guard. Why do you have to be so defensive? Nobody is attacking you. You are so difficult. Where are you from?*
—*Puerto Rico.*
—*No wonder.*

You ask me to prove discrimination. But your court of law is based on the oath: *In God we trust.* If in God you trust, then don't ask me to prove a goddamned thing. I can't prove the ghost of discrimination, but I have suffered the consequences of being haunted by that ghost. I have been misused and mistreated—undervalued—underpaid—taken for granted, not heard, not taken seriously, denied, and deprived. Even though I am pushed aside, I have a center—and my center attracts people who are in the center, but who have no center. I'm not in the center of power, but I have the center of my voice, and I will be heard. I guarantee you that. You think that what is important is the position—the substitution—so that there is not an empty chair in the room—so that nobody notices that there is someone missing—because if we start missing someone or something, problems and vendettas start appearing—because we start comparing what was with what we have now and we should not compare. Why—why can't I compare what was with what is—if what was is better than what is—or if what is is better than what was?

—Are we better off than we were 20 years ago?

That is what politicians always ask when they put their hands in their pockets and take some coins in their fists and make them ring like a bell. And they wink at you as if you were an accomplice to the crime. We are in this business together. Either we survive or we drown the stage in tears, even for an eggshell. They know and we know better—not that things are not better. Who am I to judge? And I don't care if we are better or worse. I am more cynical than that. I know better what to expect, and I also wink my eye, as an accomplice to the crime. But don't lie to me. Don't wink your eye and tell me that things are better when they are not. Or that they were better when they weren't. I see what I see with my eye—not with yours, which doesn't mean that I don't approve of your winking. I wink when you wink at me—and if you cry—I'll cry with you—but I won't lie to myself. What I see is what I see—but allow me to disagree—I like your lies—and the way you tell them I like more—because I love show business—and I love acting. There is something in this where my melancholy sits on brood. Replacing is a way of not noticing the difference, and what is important is the sameness, we are all equal with equalizers—and if you are not an equation that equalizes—you better downsize your size because who the hell do you think you are?

Righteous are those who grant themselves rights. Not only are they right, but they have the right to do what they want because they grant themselves the right. They don't doubt their righteousness.

That would be to doubt their entitlement. This is how they break walls and pass to the other side—never questioning their right of way—because their way is the right way—always right and always imposing their righteousness on anyone who doesn't think he is right. They are the makers of their righteous laws—and the lawmakers of the righteous—and with their laws they stop anyone who is not righteous. If you don't think you have the right—you will never have the right—because the first commandment is to feel the right to break the law that isn't right for you. What you'll never understand is that I don't want to be the boss—the mandatary of guinea pigs—because I am not always right—and when I am right—I start doubting I am right because my power has always been in doubting what is right. I don't understand how you can always think you are right. Maybe that is why you are so conflicted. You must really work hard on all your doubts—to keep pushing them down—as if they didn't exist—or as if they had no right to exist—because they are not convinced that you are right. The second commandment is never to apologize—even when you have done wrong—never admit wrong—because you are right to be wrong—right not to succumb—and succumbing comes when you fall into the darkness of doubt—into the perforations of conscience or consciousness—into complexities of measurement. Never weigh possibilities on scales. Never doubt. If you doubt, your enemy will enter the gates of your city.

First you destroyed my language. You broke holes in my language. You wore an inspector's cape and stuck your nose wherever there was a pocket to breathe—nosing around to see if I had weapons of mass destruction.

—All my doors are open to the inspectors. See, no weapons of mass destruction. I only want to create.

But you came and planted weapons of mass destruction. And then you told the world:

—Look! She has weapons of mass destruction!

You planted biological and chemical weapons inside my refrigerator to freeze my feelings of love, so that I would hate you and doubt myself. You accused me of your crime—playing the victim:

—Don't you see she is inflicting all those wounds on herself. Nobody is hurting her. She is hurting herself to get the attention of the world. She is crying out of pity for her own self-inflicted wounds.

Shame on you. Liar. You lied to me. You lied to the world. You came looking for yourself. You were smelling your own dirty deeds—your own weapons of mass destruction. No weapon of mass destruction ever destroys another weapon of mass destruction. What are destroyed by the weapons of mass destruction are the masses. You came looking for the dictator and you found yourself. You come from a land of mass destruction. English is a language of mass destruction. Lady Macbeth is a queen of mass destruction. Lear is a king of mass destruction. Hamlet is a prince of mass destruction. Shakespeare is a bard of mass destruction. And Moby Dick is a whale of mass destruction. Why are you a culture of death and destruction? Why do you obliterate villages, cities, and civilizations with your language of mass destruction? Is the destruction worth the destruction? For what purpose did you destroy my language? To impose the sovereignty of your rule of law with weapons of mass destruction—to then say:

—I offer you my lifesaver. Now we can communicate in the same language. English only, please.

Hierarchy of Inspiration

My hierarchy of inspiration is the daemon, the duende, the angel, and the muses. Starting from the bottom and rising up the scale from one to four, the muses are here to amuse me—and to transform my moods—from a Groucho to a Harpo—from a harpist to a trombonist—or a philanthropist—from a giver to a feeler—from a doer to a shaker of foundations of horoscopes and museums. These are the muses who amuse me, who change my moods with different shades of colored lenses in my glasses—and they are sopranos coloraturas—their tones are screechy—and I feel ticklish when I hear them coming.

Every moment has its moment—so I have to wait for the moment to come—to detect its energy—raw, medium-rare, well-done, burnt. Tones are what I hear in the laughter of the muses—high and low—indirect and direct verbs—transitory energy or high energy with green fever—and fever comes with fervor—and fervor is sustained by high doses of wind and concentration—fixed in the eye of the storm—centered in the bull's eye—to take the bull by the horns—and feel no evil eye—but break the horns of the bull called death.

Sometimes my words are poor in thoughts and rich in fantasy. Poets like to muddy the waters and then they want to see through those muddy waters. And they don't need goggles or flashlights to magnify the dirt. They see the dirty waters and they don't know what to do with the dirt—because they prefer the waters crystal clear—and only an editor can separate good from evil—clean from dirty. But the nature of the poet is to see through the mud. To throw dirt in people's faces—without distinguishing a king from a beggar. The clumps must fall where the chips do—in everybody's face—without distinction. All of them should feel the mud—and smell it—and find a sapphire in a pig's shit.

Sometimes I write and I am correcting the writing while I am writing—and thinking this is very good—and that is my vanity talking—but my modesty comes in as a voice over narration, asking—who are you? A shaken tree that is dropping a branch and giving a fruit. Too sentimental—I add. My modesty replies—you're nothing. Keep going in your endurance. A lasting moment is a syllable that crunches like Cheetos and dissolves on the tongue.

My silence has sunken—sunken into a pillow—a pillow where the ear is hearing the silence of the chicken before it ruffles its feathers and lays a dozen verbs.

The duende wants to be the daemon and break foundations—but he believes in the institution of the foundation. He has roots. He is traditional—and folkloric. He sings to his culture, to his nation. He believes in nationalities and family values—and suffers from ruptures and divorces because he wants a mistress and a wife—a cake and eat it too. His foundation is an in-between state—between the high and the low. Always question the nature of his voice when it sings very high and very low because the nature of the duende is neither to sing very high nor very low—but to perform the registers of highs and lows—because the duende chokes in his throat—that is where his roots are—in the throat—not in the head—sometimes in the stomach—he feels comfortable after a home-cooked meal. His vocal cords are strained after drinking cognac and choking on sentimentality that cracks his voice when he sings from the things he loves. He has a big heart that he heaves into his throat and he chokes on his roots.

The daemon has no roots. He has legs and he walks—pisses and shits on roots—and nourishes them too—and swings his tail while he walks—leaving those roots behind. He never creates foundations. He destroys the irremovable and jumps on gaps. He breaks the foundations of institutionalized thoughts that make the duende choke. The duende carries burdens—and when he sings you hear the voice of debt and constraint—grudges appear like hiccups and sometimes sneezes. He coughs a vengeful thought—and chokes on it with the ardor of cognac—and his face turns red as if to say: I can't go any further. This is my breaking point.

Roots should always be left behind. If you bring them to the present, you are a dead man walking. I don't want to be a dead man walking. And how do you walk when you are dead—with a chip on your shoulder—and that the daemon doesn't have—no chip on his shoulder—no dead man walking—but a smile on his face—like the smile of the smiling damned villain who surpasses the struggle of good and evil. He is not a victim of his own thoughts. His thoughts don't crowd him. He is not ticked by the chip on the shoulder of the dead man who drowns in his own sorrows which are more powerful than what he has to say, to do. That doesn't happen to the daemon who laughs with tears and breaks the chip eating Cheetos and burritos and honey and milk and lamb to remember that he overcame the sacrificial lamb—a bit of a dictator in high boots—but his pants fall and he screams—aaah. Who would have thought that he would be scared to be caught with his pants down when he has nothing to hide and he even forgot he had an ass.

Sometimes my thoughts are heavy because I am not ready. I am ready when my voice has a ghost—and I don't mean a shadow, but a double.

> *Who is the third who walks always behind you?*
> *When I count, there are only you and I together*
> *But there is a third who hovers*
> *Between our faces and slides*
> *Between the cushions.*

I make poetry with him. I count on his energy and his support of my project. Not every day is he willing to grant me graces and providences. And sometimes I walk on eggshells—fearful of breaking them—or making noise—because if I awake him when he is not ready, he will damn me with the curse of silence for two or three more months. I have to capture him when he is running ahead of his time—without letting him know that he is going to be captured. He hates captivity—and if he senses I'm trying to capture him he will run ahead of his time and leave me behind. I am always behind him, but when I walk at his side I am ahead of my time—and I sing from the top of my head—and get a headache. I don't believe that to sing from the top of the head is better than to sing from the diaphragm or the lungs. And to sing while I walk is as good as feeling free from the head—as if somebody had cut my worries off at the neck.

The daemon carries no burden—no sorrow—no remorse—no past. He held the Inquisition of Memories in the Pastoral. He laughs and cries at the same time and affirms that life is neither happy nor sad, but beautiful—and that longer than good luck is time and longer than bad luck. The daemon believes in liberty and destiny and in those things that are watching you, but you don't know where they are coming from. He believes that the moment has yet to arrive. And that he was chosen—and that he has no alternative but to follow the road that was paved for him. When he sings his eyes are fixed on that moment when alpha and omega meet.

The angel brings me the news of the world: the good, the bad, and the ugly. The angel is the messenger—that is why he has wings—to fly instead of sing. His messages are written on yellow pages and carried in a messenger bag from Hermes strapped to his back. He is always running late because instead of using his wings he rides a bike and the traffic is bad. He announces the good and bad. But longer than good luck is time and longer than bad luck. And the angel is not a messenger of good luck or bad luck, but a messenger of time. Expediency is the grace. He delivers blessings—and providence. He worries about accommodation and stipends—and how to make a living—to profit on tips—and protect the poet from self-destruction. And he also believes that fate is a creation of the mind of the poet to protect himself from evil spirits that would like to cut his life short. A fate made to end with laurels and not with accidents. Although the messenger and the bike are swift to react to accidents and lightning. The angel's mission is not accomplished until he tickles the ear of the poet with whispers and whiskers—and the poet writes down the message and this message is interpreted on different levels by the daemon, the duende, and the muses who, with their hands over their mouths, laugh out loud—but hide their laughter—and it's their duty to change the set—let the curtains fall—and turn the lights out.

Part Two:
United States of Banana

Burial of the Sardine

[There at the Fulton Market—where three roads intersect—was the point where Hamlet, Giannina, and Zarathustra first met. The three had been walking the streets like mad—without stopping to rest—until they came to the South Street Seaport—where flies were harrowing around the halo of the fish market that smelled like the rot of China-town. They recognized one another and walked toward each other with dead bodies on their backs.]

Giannina:
I'm burying the sardine—the dead body I carry on my back.

Zarathustra:
A little fish—in a little coffin. And for this—for this little stinky thing—we came from so far?

Giannina:
Look, it's moving. It's still alive.

Zarathustra:
It's so salty and ugly it itches and bites.

Giannina:
It worked its whole life in the sludge of oil and vinegar. I'll sprinkle incense, myrrh, and a pound of gold to be buried with it under the sand.

Hamlet:
Hurry up. The ferry will leave without us.

Giannina: You have no idea how much I've suffered under the influence of this rigorous but retarded sardine. Not a warrior, but a soldier. Making me vow to its regiment of passive-aggressive work. No traveling was allowed. No smoking allowed. No pets allowed. No one could get near me because the sardine would stink—and its stink would bite. Sometimes it would fly around the rim, but it would always dive back into the can of sardines—looking for its paycheck. Every two weeks—it brought me a salary—the stinky sardine—and I brought home all I could buy with that salary—confinement, imprisonment. Depending on a salary made me salivate—but it blew my mind to dust—the dust that blows around and makes you cough—but you hardly can see it because it's made of dust. But I'm not made of dust—I'm made of flesh—and making love to the little sardine drove me crazy. It was such a little fish it barely filled my mouth. I could hardly eat it. I grew hungry—hungry for a big fish. God help me—no more fish! Please no clams, no oysters! Please—nothing shelled or scaled! Nothing salted—nothing finned or fanged! Because it had fangs—the sardine had fangs—and it bit me like a rabid squirrel. It must have known I wanted to bury it. Its fangs were long—and its screams were shrill—and it held grudges—and it had bones to pick. It blamed me for keeping it down—but all I wanted was its liberation from the can. I wanted it to breathe clean air—and to sing. Your mouth is already open—now take a deep breath, little fishy, and sing—sing a song of love. You know my cords are made of vibrant colors. You know I too come from the sea—but I don't come with grudges in my fangs. I come with wings to fly from your stink. I hate sardines.

Zarathustra: Then why do you eat them?

Giannina: Because I detest their helplessness. I wouldn't eat a lion. It would eat me first. I eat what is weaker than me. I like lamb. I watch a grazing lamb, and my mouth waters. I could eat it alive. But not sardines. They're already dead. They never lived. They're dead even when they're alive. Always with their mouths open. Begging for water. And I don't mind beggars. But sardines are not beggars—they're squirmers. They beg for water—but what they really want is to eat you alive—with their deadliness—which is a plague—a virus—bacteria—something contagious that kills you without killing you. They open their mouths to beg for water—but do nothing but gulp the draught and wait for water—with their mouths open—as if snoring, which is worse than imploring—they're beggarly beggars that don't even beg—they're too dead to beg—and they're deadly contagious. It's their deadliness that lingers over me every day of my life—the dead inertia of the sardine that obeys and begs for water, gallons of water, and does what it's asked to do in spite of no water and denies itself so much—that it doesn't realize it doesn't have a being anymore—and it lets itself be canned—always with its open mouth saying:

—*Drop dead, but give me drops of water. I don't want to be buried alive. I want to survive. I'm a salaried sardine. Give me more money.*

That's why they're so salty and ugly, they itch and bite. Because they're salivating for salty salaries—salty salaried sardines.

Zarathustra: It is not a sardine. It is a big fish.

Giannina: The coffin is small, but the stench is immense. Zarathustra, would you allow my little pet to be buried in the same hole of the hollow tree where you left the tightrope walker?

Hamlet: And may I please leave the putrefied carrion in the same hollow tree?

Giannina: We are burying sameness—the aesthetic principle of sameness—the three together—at the same time—holding hands—burying bodies in the same hollow tree—and running free from freedom. Free.

Hamlet:	More myrrh, more gold, more incense—to purify the air. And there is no blood spill.
Giannina:	Not this time. This is the burial—the enclosure of the deed. This dust will purify the air. Hang in there while I finish the rites.
Zarathustra:	I have been hibernating.
Giannina:	I have been stagnating.
Hamlet:	I have been trying to figure out what I should do with Polonius's body. I might as well do what you did, Zarathustra, leave the body in the hole of a tree—but before I leave it in the hole of a tree—find a hermit to give me two pieces of bread so I can give a piece of bread to the dead.
Zarathustra:	I already left the corpse in the hole of a tree. Now I need to find the overman—somebody who rescues me from the principle of equality:

—All men are created equal.

Maybe that is why they are men because they have equal eyes, ears, and noses—and they have voices that bark. But I am looking for inequalities. My thirst is unequal. Satiety is not satiated. And it's not water I need, but networkers.

Giannina:	So, after all, you are a networker. You work the Internet.
Hamlet:	I am a fishmonger at the market smelling everything that is putrefied. I smell the stench of death—and I have not gotten to my goal.
Zarathustra:	I am still walking the tightrope—trying to get to the other side.
Hamlet:	Do you realize we are posthumous? We are talking after.
Giannina:	Speak for yourself. I'm not. Not yet.
Zarathustra:	But you don't count—with your broken English—you cut the line—you're not invited—little fox. You think you are a visionary just for saying: I am going to bury the 20th century. In 1998 you said it—and here we are in 2006—and you are still trying to bury the body.
Hamlet:	All these bodies are pestering the annals of literature. We have too many unresolved issues.
Giannina:	When I said I will bury the 20th century—everybody—not just me—went looking for a dead body. When Princess Di and Dodi died—people thought—oh, this is the funeral we've been waiting for! And when John-John Kennedy died, Americans appropriated the death

of Lady Di—and said—this is our American dead prince. But they were inconsequential deaths—deaths that were not the beginnings of a war—nor the end of a century—but accidental incidentals—and their bodies were buried.

Hamlet:

Wait a minute, the death of Polonius was an accidental death, and so was the death of the tightrope walker. And Antigona's brothers were casualties of war.

Giannina:

I am not here to analyze literary texts. You did what you did. I do what I do. What we have in common is our brotherly love—we bury bodies—and we never give birth—although I am in labor most of my life. In labor like Zarathustra. Not like you, Hamlet. You're a suicide bomber—and a camel with too many grudges. You should have been what you are—a poet—but instead the hunchback took center stage—because you were possessed by your father's ghost, which was the absence of present life in you. You did not live. You remembered. That's why you didn't have an objective correlative. What you had were regrets that you didn't become the poet that you should have been. You should have given up the crown—and followed the path of Yorick—the path of music and love. Your feelings were overwhelming—and they overwhelmed you. Why didn't you write them down?

Hamlet: Words, words, words.

Giannina: What were you reading? That is the question. Instead of writing, loving, living—in the experience that is—not in the regrettable state of what was. I don't want to fall into the pit of Ground Zero again. Why are we here? Let's state the facts of our last supper.

Zarathustra: We are gathered here to break bread with our dead bodies.

Giannina: I found my dead body in a manhole—two blocks south of the World Trade Center where I was living when the Twin Towers collapsed. Even now, they are finding bones in manholes—and as long as there are bones—I still have lines to write. I like dead bodies and leftovers. I can see clearer when nobody is looking. When everybody goes to sleep—very late at night—I see what I saw when I lived at Ground Zero. I walk like a hunchback with a knapsack on my back.

Zarathustra: Clear our purposes. Revise our expectations. Set our goals a deadline. Revisit our analysis—explore new consequences—stabilize our instability—take a piss—before we embark on our journey to hear the speeches of Segismundo, the overman.

Giannina: Not an overman. A prisoner of war, a slave of liberty.

Zarathustra:	The slave is liberty, trapped in the statue with Segismundo.
Giannina:	Talk to her. Ask for advice.
Zarathustra:	She won't listen to us. She hates us. She is a feminist.
Giannina:	She will listen to me. She is French. Do you believe in liberty?
Zarathustra:	As much as I believe in God, in Santa Claus. God is the enemy of philosophy. If God exists, why should I exist? If I exist it is to question the possibility of God. God is always trying to put a stopgap in my brain.
Hamlet:	Ghost is the absence of work.
Zarathustra:	Madness is the absence of work.
Hamlet:	What is madness but the ghost of my father. I didn't do what I should have been—a poet. The absence of work is madness.
Giannina:	Entertain me a little more while I finish my supper. What have you been doing after death?
Zarathustra:	Sleeping on laurels. Listening to the voice of critics. I can't stand what they say about me. I could never stand myself. That is why I had to disappear après my time. I could have waited longer.

But I lost patience. And faith. No, faith I never had. But patience I lost. Being alone is not easy. Always alone—without even a platonic dialogue. *Despotricando*—and preaching—always having to say something wiser than what another just said—using his argument to upset my own—to displace my argument—to take it out of context. And once my argument was taken out of context, I would always find a parking lot in that empty space where I would park my car. And give my speech—from the highest point of view. Even though blind—I could see the bridge over the cliff—and the abyss between the bridge and the cliff—and my eyes would shine more astounded than ever—looking over the ridge—at the abyss— and the cliff. Poets don't mean what they say. They take no responsibility—no accountability—they have light feet—they run like rabbits after carrots—intuitions—and leave the tortoise behind— with jetlag—and myopia and eyeglasses—studying studiously the flight of the rabbit.

Giannina: I have a lucky rabbit's foot and tortoise shell glasses.

Hamlet: I have crab legs. If like a crab I could walk backwards—and resurrect the body of my ghost— and as a crab—walk backwards—behind the tortoise crawling behind the rabbit eating carrots.

Giannina: What are carrots but flashlights of intuitions?

Hamlet: And what are flashlights but the spotlights of ghosts.

Giannina: I prefer track lights. They put me on track.

Statue of Liberty: I have inspired empires. I have destroyed empires.

Giannina: How did you become a mummy? Weren't you supposed to be a good wind that makes everything feel good? Your torch—wow—it's the spotlight over my head.

Statue of Liberty: What do you want from me?

All Three Together: Orient us. Are we are on the right track?

Statue: I am a trophy. They played a game—a tennis match—the French and American jokers at the tournament of liberty—and I became the trophy. I am the spirit of Joan of Arc. I liberated France from Anglo-Saxon freedom in the Middle Ages—and was burned at the stake. I came back to lead the French Revolution—and was sent to the guillotine. I reincarnated into the spirit of Napoleon. The French sent me to America as their horse of Troy. Under American surveillance, I've been the unhappiest woman on the planet. They turned me into the mausoleum of liberty. They say: Freedom! Freedom! But freedom means Anglo-Saxon Protestant rule oppressing the Latin, African, Asian, Arab, and Jew. When immigrants come looking for freedom, I suck their juice—under the surveillance of dread of labor without labor—of jobs without lightness of feet and creativity. I kill music. I kill love. Banks are banking my juice into credits and debts. But something is changing. I was Sleeping Beauty for too long. But life is not a dream. I have been waiting for a Prince of the Gutters to rise and seal my lips with a kiss that will awaken the winds of Joan of Arc, the French Revolution, and the spirit of Napoleon Bonaparte. With one kiss on the lips—I will come alive again. The moment has arrived. When the three come together: Hamlet, Giannina, and Zarathustra. I am already feeling the signs. My cheeks are blushing. My knees are shaking. I feel vulnerable again. This Prince of the Gutters will make love to me. I will make love to him. We will become one and bring an era of peace and prosperity. Throughout the Americas, from the tippy-top of the Yukon to the tippy-toes of la Tierra del Fuego. Let me tell you, Anglo-Saxon dominance is doomed. It wants to be the head, but it's the tail of a dog. The worst is ruling our shores.

Zarathustra: Pity the country that is ruled by the worst. And I don't pity anyone—not even the country ruled by the worst.

Statue: You don't know, Zarathustra, how many repressed emotions I've had to bury in my chest. I was almost diagnosed with breast cancer a few years ago. But I did something illegal—and if the authorities knew about it—they would have hammered me down to pennies—searching for the terrorist who sucked the milk from my tits. Since then I have not been the same—I cry, I weep. I am not supposed to feel—I am a mummy. My job is to gag and bind the prisoners of war—and the illegal aliens—and whip them into submission. But I feel for Segismundo. I nursed him. He might steal my crown one day. Unless, unless I realize I am not a dominatrix but a genie with human feelings that can love and be loved—even by one called a terrorist. Segismundo is not a terrorist, I assure you. He is a liberator.

Zarathustra: He is the overman.

Giannina: He is a poet.

Hamlet: He is a conqueror. I see him rising up from the dungeon. He will make Puerto Rico a state. Then he will become the president of the U.S. and in the spirit of Napoleon go south and conquer all Latin America.

Giannina: Again! The same mentality of domination! Can't we come up with a better system where the ones on top aren't whipping the ones on the bottom into hard labor, bankrupting creativity. Give me your social security number.

Statue: My social security number is 009-11-2001—the day the towers fell, I began to shrink.

Giannina: Is that your expiration date? I still see you standing there.

Statue:

The day Segismundo takes the crown.

Giannina:

As a product you have an expiration date. But you're not a bottle of champagne or perfume—you have the stench of sweat—you have blood on your hands—you are a revolutionary—you are change—you mean business. You weren't meant to be a product—to be sold on free markets. You don't believe in free markets or free trade agreements or freedom fighters. Marketers have misrepresented you. You've become a symbol of the establishment, but you were meant to abolish slavery—overthrow the status quo—blow winds—inspire change. Instead they bottled your essence so they could sell you. That's why you have an expiration date. Products are meant to expire. But once your genie is out of the bottle—you will become a creative process again. Your genie wants to be liberated. Who among us doesn't want liberation? We are on a quest for something higher than material dispossession.

Statue:

Can I sing again as the fat lady you've all been waiting for?

Zarathustra:

Why do you think I became a hermit? I entered the stage of the world—and my exit was fast. I gave my speeches. I said what I had to say. I gave what I had to give and when I had no more to say—silence sealed my lips.

Hamlet: The rest is silence.

Giannina: I used to hear the voice of the people in taxi drivers—but now their voices are hooked up to cell phones, iPods, or BlackBerries. If you talk to them—they disconnect only for a second—and return to their gadgets. Human beings can't bear very much reality. They need a prop in their hands. It used to be the cigarette. Everybody was smoking in the streets. And now they use electronics to formalize the fact that they're busy with the dread of daily living that produces nothing creative but the monotony that they call pragmatism. They're busy producing dust, frenemies, intrigue. They're fire-breathing dragons foaming at the office of their mouths. What would happen if we snipped the wires of their busyness. Progress would happen—as it did to us on September 11. Inspiration made an installation that day.

Zarathustra: That whirling of the Muslim world—that earthquake. We were walking with our dead bodies on our backs.

Giannina: I thought—more delays—I'll never get to the statue. But the delay turned out to be progress. I had to move from Ground Zero back to midtown again. I lost track of the Statue of Liberty and of Segismundo. Even they lost touch with themselves. Segismundo, who was milking the breast of Lady Liberty, retreated into the dungeon—receding into seclusion and silence. I said: Enough! Let's start our voyage again. We were set to take a ferry to Liberty Island when the Twin Towers melted down. I thought: Am I melting? Where is my creative energy? Where is my progress? Where is Zarathustra? In what part of the city is Hamlet? If like a crab I could walk backwards. Backwards I walked—and like a crab I found Hamlet crawling into a manhole where he thought he would find Ophelia's funeral procession—instead he found the bones of the businessman.

Hamlet: Alexander died, Alexander was buried.

Giannina: It's not over until it's over. Do you think I came to this country to shrug and say: Well, every empire has to expire.

Hamlet: Our empire is over.

Giannina: It might be over for you. But for me it has not even started. I'm starving. You ate all the food. And left me leftovers. I'm hungry. I'm an illegal alien. My strength is not satiated like yours. You might be disintegrating into body parts. But not me, honey. I am not over. It's over for you, but for me it's only just beginning.

Hamlet:	How is it that the clouds still hang on you?
Giannina:	I'm supposed to ask you that question.
Hamlet:	Why? The clouds are not hanging on me. They are hanging on you. Your eyes are not shining—they are cloudy. Is it supposed to rain, or are you going to cry tears seven times salt?
Zarathustra:	If you cry, I will not pity you. I will lose all the admiration I have acquired looking at you.
Giannina:	Why would I cry? I have no reason to cry. If tears come out of my eyes, it's because I have a runny nose and teary eyes—the pollen in the air—and the insecticides—the fumigations and the pesticides—not because I'm crying inside. I feel no pity.
Hamlet:	Look how she moves her eyes like a slot machine calculating the odds in her head. How much luck she has in the bank. Money is the motive of her mischief. My eyes move slowly like the eyes of a sage in a contemplative, meditative state.
Giannina:	I can contemplate life from the highest point of view—but right now I'm feeling low. People say I'm a screamer and a spitter—and that it's difficult to understand me. Although I am writing in English—they hear and read the foreign accent. Hamlet, you are a minority among us. Zarathustra and I are the majority. We have an extra vote. We speak English with an accent—as a second language.

Zarathustra: I run. I want to arrive swiftly. Delays bring grudges. I don't want to have clouds hanging on my fur brows or wrinkles. I am not worried.

Giannina: Of course you're not worried. You don't have to wake up tomorrow. I have to wake up tomorrow. These days I wake up in a foul mood. Why should I wake up? For what? Not that I like to sleep either. If I could, I would never sleep. I would walk wide awake even as a sleepwalker.

Hamlet: I was not given a deadline—it could have taken a month or so—instead it took years to bury what is already dead.

Zarathustra: I did not come here to bury what is dead. But to be astounded by new encounters.

Hamlet: You like brightness. I like shadows. I see the ghost in shadows. I drink coffee at Starbucks.

Zarathustra: Coffee goes with you. Coffee goes with grudges—it holds grudges—it keeps people awake who should be asleep. They are sleepy-heads who have never truly awakened—who constantly have to be reminded that they are awake—by an alarm clock or the adrenaline of caffeine—they are programmed by computers and they punch their hours. Nailed to the cross of eternal labor without giving birth.

Giannina:	Statue, how much will it cost to liberate the island of Puerto Rico?
Statue:	It's not for sale.
Giannina:	In the United States of Banana everything is for sale. Calculate per head. What is the value of each Puerto Rican?
Statue:	If a construction worker dies from asbestos poisoning, his family collects up to $3 million. I would pay $5 million. So multiply that by?
Giannina:	5 million citizens.
Statue:	You would need kabillions.
Giannina:	I'm afraid my people would say give us $5 million each and forget about freedom. Do you think we could raise the money?
Statue:	Find rich donors in Latin America. The U. S. of Banana likes to milk the cow of Puerto Rico. It won't be a popular cause here.
Giannina:	We'll stage a gala benefit. Do you have the list of major donors?
Statute:	Ask Chávez. He will donate barrels of oil. His frenemy Cisneros will give twice as much in free airtime. Though enemies they both believe in Bolivar.

The Santo Domingos in Colombia will donate a beer sponsorship. Amalita Fortabalt once offered to buy the liberty of las Islas Malvinas but never put her mouth in her pocketbook.

Zarathustra: I can't stand this conversation about money.

Giannina: You have to understand the money to understand the country.

Zarathustra: There is nothing to understand in money.

Giannina: Philanthropy. You're the most generous man on this planet. I have sucked the milk from your motley cow. I'm afraid I might have sucked it dry. How much your generosity has given me.

Zarathustra: Not money.

Giannina: If I could buy the liberty of my island, I would. If I were a kabillionaire, I would make an offer to the U. S. of B. They would take my offer seriously. More seriously than my poetry. The statue is a specialist in philanthropy. She is a fundraiser.

Statue: I am a piggybank. Immigrants talk to me about their feelings. They feel like piggybanks. But if you feel your brain is a piggybank—for God's sake—in God we trust—work harder until you become a cash machine. Your salary will increase and so will your social status when you print a business card that states your name and your new title. From Assistant Piggybank to Associate Cash Machine. Progress in this society has to do with the profession of money. Going from one profession to the other. Merit resides in your ability to count rapid sums of money. Roll your eyes blank at the *buscones* who are *buscando* money. Roll your eyes—emotionless—pitiless—no ear to them—deaf—and above all—heartless. You will not be moved by the heart—nor by graces—nor by looks. You will be moved by cash—cold—hard—cash—in money we trust. God is money. So, yes, go buy the liberty of your country. Offer the U. S. of B. more than it makes on Puerto Rico—multiplied by the number of years it has profited from the island. How long has Puerto Rico been a colony of the U.S.?

Giannina: More than one hundred years.

Statue: Well, those numbers must be considered. How much per capita has the U.S. made on Puerto Rico every year of those one hundred years—plus compounded interest—back taxes—and penalties—plus forty acres and a mule. And still, the U.S. won't be willing to let go of Puerto Rico. It's the only U.S. territory affiliated with Latin America. Puerto Rico is a public relations model. Popularity is created, and so are enemies.

Giannina: I fear Cuba is the more desirable.

Statue: It is more desirable but not more valuable. Of course, you always prefer the Dark Lady—the one who rejects you for another lover. You have better chances of becoming the lover of your enemy than the lover of your friend. There is passion in rejection—in cruelty—I know about that. I see the passion of my prisoners—they hate me—they all want to kill me—but they would all want to fuck me first—and then fall madly in love with me.

Giannina: Have patience, Hamlet. I know you can't stand corruption. But one way or another I'll negotiate my entrance into the Statue of Liberty. You two have no problems. You two are trusted. You are German. And you are English.

Zarathustra: I am not German. My stock is Polish. I have no grudges. No vengeance. I look more like Montaigne and Pascal than Goethe or Wagner. God is my body.

Giannina: Don't indoctrinate me. I'm tired of wisdom.

Hamlet: I am not English. I am Danish.

Giannina: You speak English, but you act French. That's what Sarah Bernhardt said. So cruel, so diligent, so strict—like Antonin Artaud, the artist you should have been. You were Hamlet because you didn't become the artist you should have been. But when you decided to reincarnate into Antonin Artaud—and became the artist you should have been—you went mad, really mad—because the artist didn't find an objective correlative for his art in society. Nobody understood him. But Antonin Artaud would have never contemplated suicide.

Antonin Artaud: I will never commit suicide. Being born an artist—becoming the artist I am has already killed me—society has killed me. It would be redundant to commit suicide when I live dead to life.

Giannina: Yes, he had to become what he was—an artist. And when he became the artist he was—he was confined to a mental asylum where he could count himself king of infinite space bounded in a nuthouse. But you don't need to go mad to be killed by society. Society can kill you by alienation—not giving you anything.

Zarathustra: Becoming an ascetic of the spirit can also kill you.

Giannina: And I also say Joan of Arc reincarnated into Napoleon Bonaparte. She wanted to create a nation—but she was burned at the stake—and when she was burning at the stake—she saw the bonfire—and the stake—and at that moment of burning—she raised her stakes—her ambition would not be quenched by fire—she would want more than a nation—she would rise again to unify the whole continent of Europe and become emperor. Napoleon is Joan of Arc. It's the same character—living in a different age—with a different ambition suited to the time. If I were Joan of Arc de Bonaparte I would become governor of Puerto Rico and make my island a state—and then become president of the United States of Banana—and head south to conquer all of Latin America and the Caribbean—and swoop back north to take over Canada. I could do all that—if only I could decide between three options: *Wishy, Wishy-Washy,* and *Washy.*

Zarathustra: You are dangerous like me.

Giannina: I am prophetic, revolutionary, and apocalyptic. I'm afraid the United States of Banana will end up like Hamlet at the end of the play—bodies everywhere—the king and the queen, Hamlet, Laertes, Ophelia, Polonius—all dead. Then Fortinbras enters. He didn't do anything to deserve the kingdom—it comes to him like a coup de grâce. Right now Fortinbras seems to me to have Chinese eyes. China could end up with everything—because it's not warring—but quietly building alliances—while the United States is walking like a chicken with its head cut off. Let me find that chicken a head—here—at home—here in America—here—where my friend Rubén Darío says:

If Segismundo grieves,
Hamlet feels it.

Hamlet: Why is he rising and not me?

Giannina: As a politician, you're a failure, my friend. You were born in the tower—and Segismundo was born in the dungeon. He rises from the bottom to the top—and you fall from the top to the bottom. A politician should not fall, he should rise.

Hamlet: A poet should also rise.

Giannina: But a poet rises while falling. It's the rising in the falling that makes him rise posthumously. Your destiny is to create poetry in destruction. While you destroy yourself and others—you consummate your highest destiny.

Zarathustra: It's the theory of the eternal return. You're saying that a character is a character is a character that exists before, later, and after?

Giannina: Yes, I am saying that.

Zarathustra: Are you saying history repeats itself?

Giannina: No, I'm saying Joan of Arc and Napoleon breathe the same air. I recognize the inspiration that motivates them.

Zarathustra: Ah, don't make me laugh. I'm talking to a buffoon. It's my fault. Why am I walking with the rabble?

Giannina: From the gutter of that rabble will rise Segismundo who will break out of the trophy of freedom and liberate the spirit of liberty.

Zarathustra: Romantic theory. That the body can't condense the spirit. That the spirit has to break the bottle. They are one and the same.

Giannina: Freedom is a demagogue. I am a warrior.

Zarathustra: Don't steal my thunder. The warrior is me.

Giannina: I want to liberate my island.

Zarathustra: To become a state? You are already speaking the language of the state—Washy. You washed the Wishy from the Washy.

Giannina: I washed my hands from the conformists who promote the status quo of Wishy-Washy. Language is not a promotion of ideologies. I am more Wishy now than ever before. I want independence. Why would I want my country to be part of a country that is disintegrating into body parts and walks like a chicken with its head cut off? I want the secession of Puerto Rico from the U. S. of Banana.

Zarathustra: The rabble. You come from the rabble, Statue. You too belong to the rabble.

Statue: At least something is alive inside me. Company is better than nothingness.

Zarathustra: Why do you think I went mad? I couldn't bear my thoughts any longer—I had explored the limits of myself—but I could not get to the other side—because I would have to start all over again—forgetting who I was—Van Gogh—Nijinsky. Going all the way. Giving it all. Then becoming empty. And nobody was taking care of me.

Giannina: You have me now.

Zarathustra: I can't bear very much of your reality.

Statue: I can't stand his tantrums.

Zarathustra: Make an effort. He is under your spell, under your skirt, under your control.

Statue: I don't want to control. I didn't come here looking for a job. I came here as an honor, as a feather in a cap, as a trophy, as a gift. If I were in Paris, I would be an *observatoire* like la Tour Eiffel and have a restaurant and enjoy laughter and romance. Here I have to be useful. They control my every step. I am under American surveillance. I am a laborer. I have to punch my hours. I am the slave of usefulness.

Giannina: What is your job?

Statue: To inform the government of the U. S. of B. about suspicious activities taking place in my domain. I supervise the undergrounds—the gutters, the subways, the channels, the tunnels. I was a monument to immigration. Now I'm a border patrol cop. I shed my torchlight on all suspicious activities taking place under my arms and my skirt—the smells that come out of my pits—my crotch—the sex scenes that I have presided over as a dominatrix—the helicopters that buzz around my crown—the head games that I have had to play with mafiosos—the scams—the galas—and the corruption that I let slip under my skirt. Oh, yes, that can all slide by—and the whipping of the prisoners of war into submission. My torch doesn't shine on the tax scams and the robberies. You know, I'm laissez faire. But I never applied for this government job. I am not a spy. Nor a policeman. I'm a slave of liberty. My sympathies go out to all the prisoners. I am a prisoner too.

Giannina: You are a war criminal. You should be judged by an international tribunal. How many dead bodies are in your cellar? You were supposed to protect us. You said to us—give me your tired, your poor, your hungry—and then you put us to work.

Statue: Who wants to work now? Everything is going to hell in a handbasket. Everybody wants to be the warden but nobody wants to be a prisoner. I'm #1. There is no doubt I am the boss. I am the greatest empire in the world. The only rotten one left. I have become obsolete—and my problem is that I can't admit change. But change happens regardless of my ability to admit change. Change means breaking open my piggybank and letting all the pennies out— all my little piggies. I am their service bank at their service.

Giannina: Oh, yes, you're always offering your services. As if we didn't know what your services meant. Sniffing around—to see what we are doing—to spy on us, copper. You change your lights—from red to white to blue—so that nobody recognizes you. But we already know who you are. When you say everything is under control—everything is going to hell in a hand basket—and I'll be the first one there—because I believed you. I am telling you now—one more threat to kill yourself and we are calling 911.

Statue:

If you call 911, I will claim I am a battered woman. You think you are the only one abused here? What about me? You don't think your epileptic attacks of truth don't bore a hole in my heart? You think I am not moved by your words? My frigidity is a consequence of my pain. I too want to be liberated from the daily dread of bossing around my prisoners. I too am a slave of a system that doesn't work any longer—repression, dread, and fear—with deadlines that never see the limelight of day. I am feeling heartburn—sunburn—this heat wave is killing me—my knees are starting to wobble—I feel I am going to faint.

Giannina:

Please, I beg you, stand up. We respect you. We adore you. Stand erect. Stand firm. Don't bend your knees—you'll crush us. We'll get the job done and figure out how to do it even faster. We're taking our time because we're upset—the heat—the sweat—and the hard labor—without rest—and the long hours—and the labor pains.

Statue:

If you don't turn in your work immediately—on demand—I have orders from the powers that be to collapse on you with more demands—and the threat of destroying myself will always be there—because what am I worth—if it's not my frigidity that works. My creativity is on strike, the lazy bum. Who do you think is supporting all the prisoners?

Giannina: If you freed us you would not have to support us!

Statue: If you ask me for the liberty of Puerto Rico it's because you don't know what you want.

Giannina: Why?

Statue: Liberty is poverty. You don't want to be poor. You want to be rich like me.

Giannina: What I desire most of all is to love. And I tried to love you, God knows I did. But to love you was against my better self because you never wanted the best for me. Always you wanted less of me to the extent that you denied my spiritual progress.

Statue: How did I stop your spiritual progress?

Giannina: By making me crave what I don't want or need. You made me forget who I am and who I was—and that stopped my spiritual progress. You say spiritual progress comes out of material evolution. But I say it's the opposite. And sometimes one doesn't need the other. You try to make my weakness my strength—but my weakness will never be as strong as my strength. You want to debilitate my intuition—my creative energy which is my forte—only to take me prisoner in your dungeon of liberty.

[The Statue, patrolling prisoners of war in the dungeon, lets Hamlet, Giannina, and Zarathustra sneak under her skirt into Segismundo's cellar.]

Zarathustra: Is it illegal to be down here?

Giannina: I never thought that after the Twin Towers fell, I would be under the influence of Lady Liberty—looking up and smelling her underwear.

Hamlet: Let's take it off

Giannina: What?

Hamlet: Her underwear. I bet she is a man.

Giannina: No, look at her vagina.

Zarathustra: That is where Segismundo has to slip out.

Hamlet: He is too big to fit through that hole.

Giannina: He has to fit. He is a slave. A slave has to born from the sex of liberty. How long has he been enclosed in a nutshell thinking that he is a prince? His hour has come. His time has passed. It came and it went—and slipped away—and now it's an imperative to come out. Too bad if he is too big. He didn't come out of the hole as a fetus—as an infant—he has to do it as a man. We will be midwives. We will help him.

Zarathustra:	I have a flashlight.
Giannina:	No wonder her belly was so big. I didn't realize she was pregnant. I thought she was bipolar—another case of split personality—but poor Statue—she is vulnerable—she is about to give birth. She says she is in control, but when she says everything is under control, expect chaos, anarchy. When she says:

> —*Don't worry. I'll take care of it.*
> —*Uh-oh*—I say—*what she is giving is peace of mind—what she is taking is control.*

In this country everybody is taught to be a boss—to be in control—of yourself and of others. The ones who are under control get penalized for obeying—for being led—instead of leading. Let another person be fooled. I don't want to be fooled by Lady Liberty anymore. Promises of liberty if I vote for Wishy. Wishy will not liberate me. I have to do it myself. I have to trespass the no trespassing.

Hamlet:	We could enter through the fire exit in the cafeteria. If you want a hamburger with french fries extra crispy with ketchup. And if you want to go to the ladies' room—do it now. Later you won't have time to take a piss. Zarathustra is exhausted and so am I. I didn't sleep last

night. I woke up very early—and too excited. I expect a lot of good things to happen on this trip. To liberate Segismundo from the dungeon, to declare the independence of Puerto Rico, to eliminate *la leyenda negra*, to open the doors of the Republic to poets, philosophers, lovers—to become happy—to become Hamlet (without Ophelia)—to eliminate sickness—to become healthy. To be or not to be.

Zarathustra: That is the cliché of the question.

Giannina: That was the cliché of the question. The question will no longer stand as a doubt—as broken into two parts—will I become what I should be—will I dare—once and for all—to declare my independence—once and for all—to stand apart by myself—not as the colony—the associated state of permanent indecision—Wishy-Washy—keeping things in an eternal immobility—always leaving the issue for later—as if it had to be kept secret—the secret of my independence from the U. S. of B. Puerto Rico will be what it is—what it has always been—what it will become—what it wants to be—free from freedom. Free.

Hamlet: What is that noise?

Giannina: The chains of other prisoners of war. Segismundo is not a prisoner of war. Segismundo comes from the smallest island of the Antillas Mayores—surrounded by water on all sides—isolated—in his own world—shackled—handicapped—practically a cripple in a cradle—an abortion of nature. His mother died when he was born, and his father saw this as a bad omen. If he killed his mother during childbirth, what will happen when he grows up? Confusion—chaos—revolution—the stars divined it—he will be a monster—he will kill his father too—it is better to prevent—to chain him to his cradle—to abort him in the dungeon of liberty. So he grew up thinking that he was not free—but that he could choose between three options—Wishy, Wishy-Washy, and Washy—and that his liberty would come one day—when he liberates Wishy from Washy—and stops Wishy-Washing his options away. This is the way the mind of Segismundo thinks in the dungeon of the Statue of Liberty:

Wishy:	*You are only Fú.*
Washy:	*You are only Fá.*
Wishy:	*You only wash.*
Washy:	*You only wish. And I am sick at heart.*

> Wishy-Washy: *You say I am neither Fú nor Fá. But I say I am Fú and Fá. You are only Fú. How can Fú be more than Fú and Fá?*

Segismundo's only leisure on this island—apart from thinking about his three options—is to rock in the cradle of nothingness—from side to side—from the side of Wishy—to the side of Washy—covering the options in between—Wishy-Washy—and covering his ass with pampers where he shits on himself. And a man comes in later to clean his shitty diapers. That man is Oliver Exterminator, advisor to the king of the United States of Banana, who imprisoned Segismundo in the dungeon of liberty more than a hundred years ago with the stigma of being born into a race of lazy, brutal, happy-go-lucky conquistadores who don't know the meaning of the four-letter word W-O-R-K, which means:

> *—F-U-C-K you! Keep your job! Keep your stripes! I want my independentista life!*

Apart from lazy, spics are despicable, unpredictable, and unaccountable, self-loathing violent pigs who always prefer options like Wishy, Wishy-Washy, and Washy. Instead of working their way out of anger and unemployment, they blame us for their problems. When they say:

—*At your service.*

They mean:

—*Fuck you. You bet. I'll never do it.*

When they say:

—*But my mother died.*

It's an excuse, a lie, not to decide between Wishy, Wishy-Washy, and Washy. They watch us eating hamburgers and french fries, and they crave rice and beans. They hear us speaking English, and they fork and twist their tongues into Spanglish—and they twist the twist—twisting their asses—tight. They're all a bunch of faggots. They like it up the ass. Fuck it good, mama. Ungrateful motherfucking assholes subverting the grammatical system because they don't even believe in the bitches who bore them.

Well, the bitch who bore this motherfucking-asshole died the day he was born. The bitch who bore him was a whore—a dwarf—a *boricua* whose name was Toña, *la negra*, pearl of the sea. She spread her legs all around town—the bitch who bore him—and she spread them wide open for Muñoz Marín. And that's how Segismundo was born, bastard child of the most beautiful whore of la Perla and the governor of Puerto Rico. With a pouch around his neck with a note that said:

> —This child will make the island great. This child will make the world change perspective from the point of view of the colonizer to the point of view of the colonized. This child will make what is foreign native and what is native foreign. He will undo all what his father did in the name of globalization. He will free the island from the state, the state from the nation, the nation from the continent. The United States of America will become the United States of Banana. And Puerto Rico will be the first half-and-half banana republic state incorporated that will secede from the union. Then will come Liberty Island, then Mississippi Burning, Texas BBQ, Kentucky Fried Chicken—all of them—New York Yankees, Jersey Devils—you name it— will want to break apart—and demand a separation—a divorce. Things will not go well for the banana republic when the shackles and chains of democracy break loose and unleash the dogs of war. Separation—divorce—disintegration of subject matters that don't matter anymore—only

verbs—actions. Americans will walk like chickens with their heads cut off.

Well, this story is upside-down, but that's the way that Segismundo was born—upside-down, feet first, and ass-backward. He grew up unfazed in the dungeon of liberty. His lack of liberty was born of neglected love. Distracted love. Everybody looks at him as if he were a goldfish in a fish tank, swishing his red and golden tail behind the glass that separates reality from dreams. And that's why he thinks *Life is a Dream*. He can't make connections. Connections are disconnected. They are shocking. Electrifying. They are in different drawers. And he never finds the connections. The drawers are open. And he just has to look for them, but not connect them. Or sum them up. Leave them broken and dislocated—as if crazy looking for an answer. Looking for someone or something to answer his necessities. But finding a disconnection, a dislocation in all the answers. But nobody wants answers. They want responses. But they don't respond. They play it by ear. As if answers would come by playing it by ear—but the options, like the answers, remain unanswered. And hanging on a tightrope—pending on a cord—hanging possibilities—without a clue as to what will happen to Segismundo, in chains, in pampers, in shackles—on the verge of breaking out of the dungeon and all its chains.

Under the Skirt of Liberty

[The skirt of liberty rises, becoming a circus tent. Underneath illegal activities take place. At times it looks like a turban unraveling to the sound of Arabic music coming from the inside. On the outside, the tarp takes on different shapes—a wing juts out, a shoulder, a torso, a head. Lady Liberty is busting out of the seams. Some think she is fat and over-populated, but, in reality, Liberty is pregnant. It was Segismundo who got her pregnant. Looking for an escape hole, he made love to her so many times that he got her pregnant—not because he wanted to get her pregnant or make love to her—but because he was claustrophobic and looking for a way out. And it's not as if he were an immigrant. People whose countries have been invaded invade the country that invaded theirs. What do they have that I don't have? But that was not the case with Segismundo. Segismundo did not immigrate to the dungeon of liberty. Segismundo opened his eyes to the world and found himself engulfed in the darkness of the dungeon—without having known the world—without windows to the sea—and claustrophobic.

If the king of the United States of Banana and Oliver Exterminator live in the crown of liberty—Segismundo lives in the latrine of liberty—hearing the flushing and the farting and all the partying—the galas and the luxury—and all the debauchery of lust, greed, and gluttony. Even if he doesn't know what is going on up there, he knows they are having a jolly good time—and he is not. He hears the laughter and the plumbing and the plumage too. When Oliver Exterminator is not leading fumigation tours in Israel, Palestine, Iraq, Iran, Afghanistan, and Pakistan, his job is to oversee the welfare of the dungeon of liberty—a U.S. territory where the inmates don't celebrate Thanksgiving or eat turkey. Oliver is considered a great secretary of state—decorated by the king with medals and feathers— for keeping Segismundo in the dungeon ever since he was born more than a hundred years ago. If Segismundo goes free, Oliver loses his job. So Oliver tries by all possible means to make Segismundo walk like a chicken with its head cut off. But all Segismundo has is a head and nothing to do. But chickens with their heads cut off are always rushing around stressed and distressed—from responsibilities and duties—schedules—from sunrise to sunset—always counting hours, minutes, and nanoseconds—they have no time to dwell—in themselves—or to feel—as a matter of fact—the fact that they have a life—their life is surpassed by their responsibilities to the crown, their ambition, and the queen.]

[In the dungeon.]

Segismundo:

What is yours is yours. But my experience with you is mine, only mine. After so many years living in the dungeon of liberty, hearing the stomping of boots on the ceiling—and the flushing of toilets, the farts, and belches—I can express my experience—not because you taught me—God forbid—you hardly taught me anything—except to wait with the patience of a house pet—every morning for my breakfast—and to think that you are the most generous man on earth because you bring me bananas and almonds every morning with the *New York Post*—and at night you spare me some spareribs. After a while, I wag my tail with affection whenever I see you coming—oh, he's bringing me food—food for my stomach—never food for thoughts—never food for emptiness—and devoid of affection, pride, liberty, love, justice, arms, letters. Once I grew tired of playing for you—monkey see, monkey do—I said—does this man have thoughts—or is he just a joke machine? That is when I understood that what you wanted from me was entertainment—entertainment without humor—and no criticism of your system. Criticism would imply an understanding of the abuser—and the abuser wants to continue abusing—without conscience—so there is never any bad conscience—as long as the oppressed never realize they are oppressed.

How many of us have died down here without knowing that we ever existed—that our bodies changed from infancy to old age—and that we never experienced the change of seasons—nor the meaning of the word love or justice. That we awake in the morning—and that our only option is to look at the ceiling—and think— lucky—think. You have three options:

Spanish—Spanglish—or English
Wishy—Wishy-Washy—or Washy
Nation—Colony—or State

After a while, you could lose the desire to live. But I had something inside—my prophetic soul that kept me crawling between heaven and earth—like Hamlet—the only book you kept shoving under my nose—but other stories rained from the skies—and music—the music of the times seeped through the walls—as new prisoners of war came from other countries— and brought me thoughts and desires and an appetite to live. And when I heard about the Twin Towers falling on your head, I couldn't have been sadder. I was really scared. What's going to happen to me now? Am I going to lose my only contact with the world? Who is going to bring me breakfast in bed? We were all won- dering—all of us—full of fear and suspense. We receded into seclusion—afraid to talk to our Arab inmates. But they always referred to me

as their American friend, the only American
friend they had in the dungeon:

> —*You have an American passport, my
> friend. With that passport you can get
> out of here. You are set for life. Segis-
> mundo, what are you doing here? You
> could become president of the U. S. of
> Banana if you sell your soul to the devil. I
> am an agent of the devil.*
> —*From what circle of hell do you come?*
> —*Hell is hell—there are no circles—but
> osso buco—empty of meat. You tuck
> yourself in the buco of the bone and wait
> for the gates of heaven to open—although
> if you have hope—you are not in hell—
> but in hoping to be in heaven—but still
> the hole is empty—and the sleeping cells
> are vast. Get out of here as soon as you
> can and take us all with you.*
> —*How?—I said. I am useless. You don't
> understand. You all came here after you
> had some control in the world. You were
> married, you were a provider, you knew
> how to swim, how to dance. You had sex,
> you had love, you had guns. Some of you
> have even killed. You've been accused of
> crimes you might have done or not done.
> But I was born here. I've never been
> outside. I've never done anything. And I*

am terrified. Because I don't know how. I don't even know how to apply for a job.
—Your problem, my friend—a Pakistani student told me—is that you've got too many thoughts bottled up inside. You need to get your head unscrewed.
—Yes, but how? How can I get out of here? We all want to get out of here, but we look at the walls—high as the owl on a scarecrow—and say: how? How? I don't know how. And even if I knew how I don't know if I would be able to do it. And don't think for one second that I'm a coward. I am capable of heroic acts. I am a hero, but I simply don't know how. Why are you all laughing at me? Because I don't know how? But you like me. I like you too.

We developed a camaraderie. They knew I would never betray them. They felt comfortable with me. We used to have dinner parties—all of us in the dungeon together—eating the leftover bones that the crown threw to the dungeon—and we chewed those bones like dogs under the table. And the more prisoners of war that entered the dungeon—the merrier we became. To the extent that a whole population—a whole city—a whole state—bigger than New Jersey— was living under the skirt of Lady Liberty— where the best smells came from her vagina— mixed with the smells of leftover scraps that were thrown to the dogs. Sometimes I think that all you need is love to be happy—and when I felt the camaraderie I felt the solidarity I had never before felt in my life. They used to say:

> —*You're gullible—you'd believe anything we tell you.*

And some of them were cruel to each other, but to me, never. The very sight of me, I don't know why, always made them laugh:

> —*The sun came out. Now we have something to talk about.*
> —*What a nut, a chock full of nuts.*
> —*So what crime are you accused of?*
> —*Just the crime of being alive—and not knowing how to get out of here. I know I will get out—but I've not finished thinking my possibilities. I am thorough. I think of all the ways—without knowing which is which, or which is better. But I will.*
> —*Yes, you will.*
> —*Yes, we can.*

The funny thing is—I was becoming their leader. Maybe because I could move them to tears and laughter, but also because I was thinking—and they saw that I was not joking—that I longed to bask in the limelight of the day—and gain relevance in this world. Like all of them.

I heard their stories. I didn't understand half of what they said, but I kept listening. They thought I was an idiot savant and humored me with love—and as long as people loved me—I was happy. If the Twin Towers hadn't fallen, I would have never met a Pakistani, Iraqi, or Iranian friend, or a Chinorican, or an Egyptian. I am thrilled to be able to talk to prisoners of war from around the world. It's becoming a gathering of tribes—a United Nations—without nations—not the whore of the U. S. of Banana—but a think tank where new ideas are brewing in the cauldron of races and genders and religions.

Sometimes the dungeon of liberty looks like the black paintings of Goya—all those faces of color. I would have never thought that I had a color until a skinhead taunted me:

> —*You're the color of night—and I am the color of day.*
> —*You're fucked up, man, really fucked up to be looking at people as chocolate bars. That's why you don't see.*
> —*What don't I see?*
> —*No, man—you don't see what is coming.*

Then all the other prisoners surrounded him. They would have beaten him up if I hadn't stopped them:

*—Yo, bro, we're all ugly, Catholic, and
sentimental. You've got the luck of the
Irish. You're lucky to have me in between.
They would've eaten you alive, brother.
Open your mind. Open your heart. Don't
be a bully. There are more things in
heaven and earth than are dreamed in
your philosophy.*
—Like what?
*—Like miracles—like changes of power—
like changes in climate—like political cli-
mates collapsing like polar ice caps—like
the dungeon becoming the crown and
the crown the dungeon—like not paying
attention to bullies—like superpowers
running out of fuel—like finding oil in
the dungeon of liberty—like the dungeon
of liberty becoming a gold mine—like
useless poets changing the way the world
thinks and sings—like a voice coming
out of the dungeon—a useless voice that
has something to say but doesn't know
how to market it—like finding yourself
for the first time happy—even though
you're in prison. Like finding camaraderie and solidarity among friends you
never thought could be your friends. Like
understanding the other—not loving the
other—but putting yourself in the shoes
of the other—not to take their position—
not to steal what the other has—but to*

*feel what the other feels—to appreciate
his thoughts. Not to be ironic—clever—
smart—but to be profound—not to be the
boss who puts everybody down—but to
be the leader of a chorus of voices—each
and every single one of them having their
own point of view—like saying—stop
being a predicate and become a subject.
—Ain't this Frenchy faggot funny? Saying
we're all ugly, Catholic, and sentimental.
—Except the Muslims and the Jews. We
all used to live together in the middle
ages in Spain—but some witchcraft broke
the enchantment of camaraderie—and
now we're boiling in the cauldron of the
dungeon of liberty.*

* * *

*—How did you sleep last night?
—Hardly—the cat was meowing.
—Which cat?
—The Statue of Liberty's cat.
—I didn't know the Statue of Liberty had
a cat.
—Yes, a Jewish cat.
—And I didn't know cats have religions.
—Maybe not in other countries. But here
cats have religions—or belong to a race.
And the Statue of Liberty's cat is a Jewish
cat.*

—*How do you know it's a Jewish cat?*
—*By the way it meows. I shouldn't have
told you it's a Jewish cat. I only told you
because you're Jewish and maybe you
could keep this secret. Let not the secret
police above the Statue know that the
Statue of Liberty's cat is Jewish. The secret
police dog is a German shepherd. Let
not the terrorists under the Statue know
the Statue's cat is Jewish. They'll stick
explosives in the cat's ass and blow him to
bloody fur balls.*
—*That Statue must be a witch if she has
a cat. And she must be a Jewish witch.*
—*No, a Jewish dragon lady.*
—*You mean a Jewish princess?*
—*No, a Jewish dragon lady. She is a mixture of races and genders. But genders
like genres are melting like seasons. The
borders are no longer effective in under-
lining distinctions. Between melodrama
and drama. The only thing that is distinguishable is religion. How thick are the
walls between cultures. I need windows
to peek through. But I am not a spy. I
live among the fragments, the torsos, the
hands, the body parts of every culture. I
eat their leftovers—and their bones I suck
to the core of my liberty.*

* * *

A suicide bomber asked me:

>—*Are you ready?*
>—*Ready for what?*—I said.
>—*For the explosion. Do you want to live
>forever under the volcano? Or do you
>want to be the eruption of lava? To have
>relevance and weight. To be all over the
>news. They say Osama Bin Laden was a
>CIA agent. They told him—if you let us
>say you did it, we'll grant you a pardon.
>We'll never find you. We'll look the other
>way. You'll become a ghostly apparition.
>You'll never be caught. You'll be a legend
>in the Arab and the Western worlds.
>You'll work for us as our enemy. Segis-
>mundo, do you want to be part of us?*
>—*Part of what?*
>—*Who are you willing to betray?*
>—*Nobody—not even you—and you
>would be the only one I would betray—
>for having betrayed me by asking: who
>are you willing to betray? I am not will-
>ing to betray anybody, not even you,
>betrayer. I wouldn't betray anybody. I
>love Arabs. I love Americans. I love Ger-
>mans and Jews and Canadians too. The
>bolts of confinement are breaking loose.
>My nails, the nails that you nailed into
>the back of the bed—to keep me down—
>are all falling down. Down with the*

dungeon of liberty. Down with the divi-sions that keep putting us down. Si, we can. Yes, se puede. Yes, we can.
—What can you?
—Yes, we can. I don't know how. But we certainly can. And we will. Yes, we will break the divisions between genres and genders and races. Fuckers. You will not divide us anymore. Yes, we will. Yes, we can—the voice of the people is breaking down the doors of the dungeon.
—Segismundo, fly, you have an American passport. Save your ass.
—Not if I can't save your asses too. All asses are worth the same. All of you with me and me with all of you. Yes, we can. Yes, we will.
—Will what?
—Break the chains of oppression. Liber-ate ourselves from the dungeon of liberty.
—When?
—That I don't know. Time is relative. I've been here more than a hundred years try-ing to break the manacles on my wrists—and the ball and chain on my ankles. The prison is overpopulated—and I am the oldest inmate—one of the originators—or primogenitors. I feel it will be soon. Too many of us are gathered here. Too many tribes wishing for the same. Portentous things are happening. Inane things—they

*just found out that the Statue of Liberty's
cat is Jewish. The secret police want
to send it to the gallows. The Statue is
shrinking.* Le chat *is mewing. Portentous
things are happening. One of the prophecies said when they find out the truth
about* le chat, *the Statue will shrink.*
—*And then what?*
—*The next prophecy will come true.*
—*Which is?*
—*When the three come together to visit
the Prince of the Gutters—*quítate tú, pá
ponerme yo.
—*Which means?*
—*Somebody will have to step down for
someone else to step up to the throne and
steal the crown.*
—*I didn't know the oracle spoke Spanglish.*
—*He spoke in tongues like all prophets
do—they see the past, the present, and
the future—all happening at the same
time—all speaking in tongues—with
tongues of fire. Prepare yourself. Be on
alert. It will happen. Like a coup de
grâce. Good things happen when they are
willed by the masses that are asses—said
the Nuyorican poet Pedro Pietri—one of
the many who died pushing the columns
of the dungeon of liberty.*

Before I used to write my thoughts on the walls of the dungeon. But now my thoughts are becoming universally known. Everybody knows that I'm in confinement. And I feel like I'm menstruating. On alert. And ready. Like a soldier who spends most of his time waiting. And when the act finally happens, it happens very fast. Like the destiny of philosophers. All their lives they are waiting for their death. And when it finally happens—it happens so fast they have no time to reflect. So, why so much preparation for reflection—when at the end your reflection becomes the act of death? *Soñemos, sueños, soñemos. Que los sueños, sueños son.*

Segismundo:	*China comunista,* my apple, my April, mixing memories and desires, with you I can really negotiate. Where are you from?
Giannina:	I was born in Naranjito.
Segismundo:	Where is Naranjito?
Giannina:	I don't know.
Segismundo:	A town? A country? A city?
Giannina:	I was born after distinctions were made. Naranjitos don't know how to distinguish. We use words like north and south. But where the north is—or where the south is—we don't know. I do know I was born in Naranjito, an island of Puerto Rico, and I'm called *Boricua.*
Segismundo:	You have the face of *una china mandarina.*
Giannina:	My mother *es china.* My father, Irish. My father used to say my mother was a trophy he won in a battle in North Korea—and he brought her as a souvenir to the island of Naranjito—a district of Aibonito on the continent of Puerto Rico which has as many states as the U. S. of B. It has Aibonito, Ay Dios Mío, Cabroncito, Cubismo, Modernismo, Curacao, Brasilia, Santiago, Argentina. It's such a big place that it has a north and a south, but don't ask me which way is which. I

didn't go to school where distinctions are made. I was born in the era of entertainment. My parents came to Puerto Rico to avoid taxes. And there I was raised by TV. Distinctions are made to make me feel small. I don't know how to cook. I don't know how to swim. I don't know how to drive. All I know is how to sing:

♫ *Oliver Exterminator*
Entonando esta canción
Oliver Exterminator
Es por siempre el campeón.

Puerto Ricans have trouble making decisions. Why decide between Wishy, Wishy-Washy, and Washy? They are all washing their wishes. They wish a deus ex machina would whisk away all their traumas of being belittled by the superpower, of being under surveillance and control, of having to make a living, for others to take their money, of not knowing how to make a living—but of knowing how to live. While Americans have a trauma between doing and being. They think that what they do is not who they are—they do the killing for a living—but they are not killers. Less important for an American is who he is than what he does. Puerto Ricans feel it's better to be conquered by a conqueror than to be exterminated by an exterminator. If you ask them to choose between an exterminator and a conqueror, they prefer to be vanquished, and that's why they choose Wishy-Washy. If you ask them: hot, cold, or warm water—warm, for them, has the vacillation and melodrama of *Estado Libre Asociado*, which is neither a nation nor a state, but Wishy-Washy. But they always have to hide their heart of liberty which beats to the rhythm of:

> *Puerto Rico, Free*
> *Puerto Rico, Wishy*

Beating in the poverty of their sad hearts is the bitterness they inherited from Spain, the wicked stepmother who was a bad mother but a mother nontheless. Whereas the U. S. of B. is neither a mother nor a father—with him we speak eye to eye—he is a crook—a thief of natural resources, a bankrupted banker, but a brother, a rebellious brother, the only one who liberated himself from his colonizers. Latin America is still living under the Spanish yoke—it hasn't sent Spain off to war to defend it. England went to Iraq to defend the U.S.— even though she knows that her son is a bipolar liar with a destructive nature. She sees him with teary eyes—I mean, he is worse than she is, but where did he learn all his dirty tricks and destructive behavior—from England. Though England feels shame, she still defends her child because she is retired and he supports her economically. Something Latin America has not done yet—support its mother economically and colonize the colonizer.

I am neither in favor nor against. I see the pros and the cons. Both sides of the same coin. Because, in the end, neither has been good to me. The first was a conqueror who taught me to scream and abuse my children the way my mother abused me. The second was an exterminator, who in some sense softened my features and lightened my load. I laugh a lot—and I've learned to be more superficial—but nothing can rid me of the atavistic complexes I got from *la madre patria*—not even plastic surgery.

Though Oliver Exterminator smoothed away my wrinkles and hushed my tone—because he doesn't like it when I scream—I'm still waiting for him to dominate me with a sense of ownership. But he doesn't want to possess me. He doesn't force me to speak his language. And to a certain point I like to be forced. That's how I was raised—to believe love is strict. And that's why I'm a little confused like Mariquita Samper, the sad colony. But there is a difference between Mariquita Samper and me. I've lived twenty more years under the regime of Oliver Exterminator, who insists I am free to do whatever I wish. The difference is that I hardly wish I were who I was when I was Mariquita Samper—because my desires have died—some with age—

not with abuse—because he treats me well, so well, I hardly feel how poorly he treats me, and that's why I don't notice the bad—because there is simply no treatment, indifference. I do whatever I damn well please. But what do I do when I have no desire? I do nothing. He killed my desires, including my desire to be Puerto Rico, Free. Puerto Rico, Wishy. To the point that I no longer find the being that I was in who I am. But Oliver tells me:

> —*Your being doesn't exist. What exists is what you do with your being. Not what you are. What you are doesn't exist. The proof that you don't exist is that you don't have a job. You're unemployed. A welfare recipient. A cockroach. Uncle Sam will send me to exterminate your desires— your being—with a fumigation. Jobs exist. What you call your being—that's all you have got left from Spain. Exterminate it to become American.*

The first thing Oliver asked me when he met me was:

> —*Oh, you don't wear pointy shoes with high heels.*
> —*Why would I wear pointy shoes with high heels?*
> —*You're a spic.*

—What's a spic?
—A cockroach kickin' Rican. You're sup-
posed to wear high heels with pointy
shoes to kill cockroaches. You live in a
dungeon with cockroaches. Where are
your pointy shoes? Are they in the closet?
Let me enter your closet. Let me see your
pointy shoes with high heels. If you don't
have pointy shoes with high heels, you
need an exterminator.

♫ *I am Oliver Exterminator*
Entonando esta canción
Oliver Exterminator
Es por siempre el campeón.

I let Oliver enter my closet to look for my pointy shoes with high heels. He wanted to know if I was capable of killing cockroaches. He didn't find any pointy shoes with high heels, but then he said to me with the smile of the villain on his face:

—Are you in the closet?
—What do you mean? Of course I am
in the closet. You asked me to open my
closet. To look for pointy shoes.
—You must have pointy shoes with high
heels.
—No, I don't. Don't you see, I don't.

—Then, how come you don't have cock-roaches? Either you have pointy shoes with high heels or an exterminator who fumigates your closets.
—No, I don't have either.
—Then you must be gay.
—This is ridiculous. Who the hell are you?
—I am Oliver Exterminator. I came here to fumigate your closet. But since you don't have cockroaches or high heels with pointy shoes, you must be gay.
—I really don't see the connection, but if you insist.
—I like you. I want to fumigate your whole house.

And he did fumigate my house—invading and pillaging all I had—even my name—taking it out of place—displacing my fame—until I lost track of myself—and became estranged. That is part of the extermination process. He called it a procedure. Not an operation. A procedure. I just had to sing along:

♫ *Oliver Exterminator*
Entonando esta canción
Oliver Exterminator
Es por siempre el campeón.

I had such a beautiful voice that all the spics
opened their doors when they heard me
sing, and Oliver became a champion for real.
Before he was just the champion of propa-
ganda. But when I sang, I was the Pied Piper
of cockroaches. His career took off with me.
He became the greatest of all exterminators.
And it was my voice that made everything happen. My voice opened all the doors for him to
fumigate. My voice was full of sun, salsa, and
merengue. But after witnessing so many exter-
minations, I became depressed—and my voice,
hoarse and shrill. I couldn't sing anymore with
the joy of the sea and the sun. No, my jingle
for Oliver Exterminator started to sound like
the Tasty Freeze truck. Then Oliver didn't like
me anymore. Because he couldn't use me. I
thought I was elevating the spirits of my people.
But I was used to exterminate them. And now
I hate myself. Oliver taught me to hate myself
the way he hates himself. He wants everyone
to hate themselves. After I discovered who
Oliver really is, a hater, I couldn't get over the
fact that I was known all over the world as the
voice of the exterminator. I decided to become
a passerby. If you can't love, just pass by. I suffered nausea. I suffered withdrawal syndrome.
I withdrew from the culture of Oliver Exterminator. I walked and walked, trying to alleviate
my spirit—but I couldn't get that tune out of my
head. That tune that I used to sing with so much

joy. And that he considered me a cockroach killer because the first thing he asked me when he met me was why I was not wearing high heels with pointy shoes. This I can't forget, nor can I forgive myself for working for the killer of my joy. For letting him bury my song and my poetry.

Segismundo: You're not the only one who was born after divisions were made.

Giannina: I didn't say divisions. I said distinctions were made.

Segismundo: And what difference does it make? The Berlin Wall came tumbling down, and so did Jack 'n Jill. Tower One came down and broke its crown and Tower Two came tumbling after. Destruction happens very fast. But look how slowly creation happens. I'm planning to build a bridge from the Mississippi to the Amazona and call it the Missizona—and millions of people will cross it from north to south and vice versa. Wherever a thought stands tall and alone—I will flap my tongue that has a flag—a flag of pride—that speaks Spanglish like the Missizona. And the citizens of Puerto Rico and New York will be called Nuyoricans. And the citizens of Chile and Argentina—Chiletinos. And the citizens of Venezuela and Canada—Canazuelans. And Arizona will not be arid but humid.

Giannina: Barriers will always exist.

Segismundo: Mental blocks will disappear. I will rub Alad-
                din's lamp like the belly of Buddha and build
                a bridge between the two Americas—a bridge
                without one loose screw or one loose cannon—
                a bridge that will build bridges and burn bridges
                at the same time.

Zarathustra: You are not the overman?

Segismundo: No, I am not over. But over me a bridge will
                be built—a bridge between man and over-
                man—between two nationalities that become
                one—and one nation that becomes many—and
                a city that becomes bigger than a nation—and
                a nation that becomes smaller than a region—
                and a nation that becomes irrelevant to the geo-
                graphical boundaries that are *passé composé*.

Giannina: This is my dirty secret. I was born after the dis-
                tinctions were made, so I don't distinguish *la
                chicha y la limonada, el merengue, y el coquí.*
                The stakes are running high.

Zarathustra: Correct, the tabs are running high.

Giannina: I can't buy the stakes because they are too expen-
                sive. But I can mistake my stakes for states. And
                states of the union are states of the union—but
                there is also a State of the Union that is a speech

that doesn't hold the stakes high—and that has an axis of evil dividing the world between good and evil, races and genders, and genders and genres.

Hamlet: How do we break the chains?

Giannina: Crack open the axis of evil. It's in the spinal column of the Statue of Liberty.

Zarathustra: If we break her spinal column—she'll come tumbling down.

Giannina: No, she will strike a new pose—more gracious and agile. I need a hammer to crack it wide open and break the wicked spell of the axis of evil. The nails will fall out one after another. Good will arrive soon. The election lights on Segismundo.

Hamlet: I said the election lights on Fortinbras.

Giannina: But look, it lights on Segismundo. Look at the halo. The halo rises when the crowd unites in one voice that becomes the voice of the individual claiming its voice through the crowd. I don't mean a leader who stands up for the rest of us. We are no longer the rest of us. We have been the rest of the world for a very long time— standing in a very long line of protestors waiting for a change—a change that never comes when

I give you one dollar and you give me back four quarters. It's the economy of divisiveness. You divide them among the tribes of quarters—so they count the quarters—and they start thinking in dimes and nickels and pennies—that bring penuries—and forget they had one dollar each. What can I do to improve the level of my audience?

Zarathustra: Don't read to them. Don't show them your work. Don't think of yourself as a performer.

Giannina: I never think of myself as a performer.

Zarathustra: But you say: I am Hamlet. And you know you are not Hamlet. I would never identify with Hamlet.

Giannina: You are not an actor. You have no empathy.

Zarathustra: You both drown in a glass of water—quenching your thirst in your pool of tears. Beyond tears and laughter—beyond the moving of emotions—is there a thought. That you can make me cry—without having any contact with my emotions. That I can laugh and have no relation to the joke. It's making me more distant to myself. For lack of control over emotions and feelings. For staying in that intermediate state— intercepting feelings—anonymous feelings—

contagious obsessions that don't rise to the level of thoughts.

Giannina:

But as you predicted that the poet will grow wary of his spirit—and that he is in danger of becoming an ascetic of the spirit—I predict the rise of philosophy and of your race.

Zarathustra:

You are still stuck in the mud.

Giannina:

You think in the bootblack, in the wisdom of the streets, there is no wisdom—only street smarts—and the poor and thirsty don't understand. You named them rabble with disdain. I love the rabble. And this is what you hate of me—that I can dance with the rabble and say I love you and you love me—when I should reject them and distance myself from that common feeling of brotherhood. And I loved your jubilation when you joined the crowd. You were right there with them—and then you turned on them—and I love that you turned on them. You say that what makes me part of the rabble is that I love your movements instead of your wisdom—and that I love the tight squeeze—standing too close to breathe—under the stand of so many others—and not rising above their understanding—instead of doing what you do—using us as stepping stones to rise to the highest cliff of the highest mountain—looking down at the rabble and saying how far you have risen—and how little is the world.

Zarathustra: The grass is always greener after the buffalos shit.

Giannina: I never cared for an audience. Publishers ask me: who is your audience? Who do you write for? I write for Zarathustra and Hamlet—this will be my answer. I don't care for an audience. Books don't have auditors. They have readers— Argos—who see. Readers don't see. Auditors don't listen. I want to be understood.

Zarathustra: When are you planning to finish your book?

Giannina: When you and Hamlet shut up.

Zarathustra: Translating feelings into thoughts. And if the feeling dares to think—and lately your feelings have shown a tendency to think—but your audience is against the thoughts of your feelings— so you step into the manure of buffaloes and cows—you prefer their company—than to have nobody around—and that lowers your standards of expectation. See if you can get a thought— a reflection, wisdom, out of a feeling, out of a tear.

Giannina: Why do I have to get anything? When I get something it's usually change—the change of a dollar into four quarters. The amount of tears stay the same—and they drop like coins.

Zarathustra: Keep the dollar—don't change it into four quarters. You spend one quarter—and you forget you had a whole dollar. It cannot be the inventors of new noise who rule the world. It must be the inventors of new values.

Giannina: Nowadays the inventors of new values need trumpets and bagpipes to announce their values.

Zarathustra: No, it decreases the value to be announced. Beware—if a new noise runs at the side of a new value and tells the new value—we are running mates—you know then that the new noise wants to steal from the new value its name—and the profit that the new noise makes decreases the value of the new value. When a new value appears, the new noise is always there to steal the name of the new value: it names it great event.

Giannina: Can't there be a work of art that is a great event and that at the same time creates a new value? You say the great event is bellow and smoke— and when it passes you realize nothing has changed. But why do you call that a great event if you know that's not a great event? I know you are being ironic. But don't define the great event as a negation of what people consider a great event—don't say: this is not a great event. Say what the hell a great event is. The great event is the creation of a new value—a new value that appears like a rainbow with many envelopes that shed mystery—and you open the envelopes and there are messages inside—and letters—and signs—and those signs transform new noises into new values.

Zarathustra: Wait, a new noise can't create a new value.

Giannina: A new voice in poetry, a poetry that takes back the thought you created—and brings that thought back to the level of intuition. You foolosophers steal the new values from poets. But since poets are peacocks who spread their tails—indiscriminately—not judging who is watching—a philosopher always sneaks into the audience of buffalos and cows to steal the peacock's rainbow and make it a new value—and he makes it inaudibly—because you know who you are—you are a philosopher. But I don't know who I am. I am a poet. All my poetry is about asking cows and buffalos: who am I? And they nod: yes, yes, yes. That's who I am. An affirmation. A dawn that is constantly making an inauguration cutting ribbons with a scissor. But when I present myself to my audience and spread my tail with that multitude of eyes that peacocks have—it's because I already know that I am a peacock presenting as my great event: a rainbow. They just have to recognize: look, there is the peacock opening her buffalo wings that are a rainbow.

Zarathustra: You would deceive a doctor.

Giannina: I would not tell a doctor my truth. Let him find it himself. If he asks me—how do you feel? I'll say—I feel fine—even if I feel bad—I'll say fine. If I tell him I feel bad, and he finds something bad—then I induced him to find the bad. But if I say—fine. And he tells me—fine, get out. Better for me.

Zarathustra: You would deceive a doctor.

Giannina: I go to Starbucks and ask for a small cappuccino. The barista says: tall. And I say: small. I know what tall is. But when I ask for small he gives me tall. Deceiving is insisting small is tall.

Zarathustra: You would deceive a doctor.

Giannina: It's like saying: ask not what your country can do for you but what you can do for your country. If I elect you—the election lights on you. So it's not what I can do for you, but what you can do for me. What kind of doctor are you—if I can deceive you? Why would I help a doctor find something bad in me? I would not help anybody find something bad in anything. I would help them find something good.

Zarathustra: You would deceive a doctor.

Giannina: If a doctor wants to search me for weapons of mass destruction, when I have no weapons of mass destruction—no—I would not help a doctor find weapons of mass destruction—when I have no weapons of mass destruction. So, yes, I would deceive a doctor—if he says—I have when I don't have. I will affirm—I don't have.

Zarathustra: Do you have words? Do your words belong to you?

Giannina: No, my answer is no. I have no property in the dictionary. Words are anonymous like the disenfranchised masses that haven't been weighed—or named—or framed. My words belong to those who don't belong. If I have a thought—I'm not the one who discovers that thought—because I'm not observing the spectacle of birth—I'm giving birth—so—if in my birthing of multiples—I give birth to something precious that catches your attention—and opens your imagination—I'm not the one who discovers it. I wouldn't know how to choose the good puppies from the bad puppies. I can't be choosy—I have to continue giving birth. The choosy one is you. You name them—you distinguish them—you select—and you separate them. I embrace them, feel their vigor inside me, and fill them all with jubilation. I can't distinguish one from the other. Later, as time goes by, one of them becomes memorable—what he says has a meaning that captures my honey—then I know that's the one who has qualities—then I name him: Zarathustra—that's the one who keeps haunting my imagination. He is the one who makes me go over each and every line. He has words. So your question is: do I have words. And my answer is: Yes, I have verbs. I lay eggs.

Zarathustra: You write to feel good. I write to find truth. I would not deceive a doctor if I were feeling bad.

Giannina: But I'm not feeling bad at all. I just went for a checkup—hoping he doesn't find anything wrong—and wanting to always feel good—hoping that I never have to see a doctor again in my life.

Zarathustra: I am a doctor.

Giannina: That's why I try to deceive you. But nobody can deceive Zarathustra. Not even Zarathustra can deceive Zarathustra.

Wedding of the Century

[On a ferry.]

Onlooker: This will be the wedding of the century.

Onlooker: It will unite South America and North America.

Hamlet: What a queer idea. I will destroy the marriage. Again! The bitch who bore me is again in heat! This is too much. I thought history doesn't repeat itself.

Giannina: History is not repeating itself. Your mother is not marrying the same man.

Hamlet: She is marrying the king again.

Giannina: But not an English-speaking Danish king.

Hamlet: A Spanish-speaking Polish king. Why does she have to marry again? That is the question.

Giannina: So that you can be Hamlet again.

Hamlet: And now that I am happy sailing toward the Statue of Liberty—talking to you and

Zarathustra—contemplating life from the highest point of view—from the point of view of the skull—from the point of view of the ghost—from the point of view of the body—and all of a sudden—I see my mother on the bow of the ferry dressed as a bride. My blood runs cold. What is she doing here? I am traveling to America to escape from her most pernicious influence. And here she comes again! The bitch who bore me is again in heat!

* * *

Gertrude: Please, Giannina, do not tell Hamlet I am here.

Giannina: I'll try, but I've never been good at secrets.

Gertrude: Basilio wants to marry me. What can I do? Two generations have different plans. Your generation thinks that the daughters and sons can replace the mothers and fathers. We will never be replaced. While you think you are here *(she puts her hand at the level of her breast)*, we are here *(she raises her hand to the level of her eyebrows)*. We will always be on top of all of you children. We have a higher purpose than you. We will unite the Americas in the name of global warming. We will warm each other's colonies in the name of old Europe. Not in the name of America. What you don't understand is that these are our colonies—the colonies of

England and Spain—and we want them back, not in the name of our sons Hamlet and Segismundo—but in the name of the father, the mother, and the holy Ghost—in the name of Empire of the old.

* * *

Onlooker: I think it's disgusting. Two old bags competing for the wedding of the century.

Onlooker: Every wedding of the century ends in shackles and chains. When are these two old rags going to allow their children to have power instead of shitting on their heads?

Onlooker: When bird shit lands on your head, it brings good luck. I wouldn't be surprised if it turned out to be a good omen. These old fuckers never gave them a chance. They saw Hamlet, Giannina, and Zarathustra coming to liberate Segismundo—and they plotted their overhasty marriage. It was probably the Statue who tattled on them. She can't help it—the nature of the beast is to betray for pay—she is a traitor turned mummy—a Horse of Troy.

* * *

Hamlet: Oh God, the bitch who bore me is again in heat! Again!

Giannina: You are overwhelmed by her. She has bewitched you.

Hamlet: The family circle bites my tail!

Giannina: Just don't pay attention to her.

Hamlet: Again! She wants to overpower me! And they name their marriage: global warming. As if they were warming the heart of the world. And their slogans are tongues of fire. This is too much, this is too, too much. The cruelest people in the world posing as warming the world, as giving sunlight to the world. It's global warning. It's a warning to the world—their warming. They are using the image of the sun—full blown—and on one side of the sun appears Gertrude, my mother, and on the other, Basilio, Segismundo's father. The wedding of the century that will warm the hearts of the world—uniting the colonies under one sun—the global warming—and in the image you see the sun melting—and they are melting too—in the cunning greed of their lustful hearts—using the climate of pollution for their political ambition.

[Gertrude meets Segismundo for the first time in the dungeon.]

Gertrude: Your father does not like you because you are too needy.

Segismundo: Can you tell me what I need?

Gertrude: You are useless. People do not like people who need. People who need people are not the luckiest people in the world.

Segismundo: What people do I need?

Gertrude: You need people to do everything for you. Why should your father have to support you at your age? I can tell you from my own experience what I do not like about Hamlet—he is too needy. Ophelia does not like it either. We used to talk about it. Why does he need us so much? Why doesn't he rely on himself? He is so needy he needs the ghost to support his madness. Or he needs Horatio. Or he needs Laertes—or me. And you are the same way. You are too needy.

Segismundo: How am I needy?

Gertrude: You are useless. You do not know how to get out of here. You need your second mother to ask your father to forgive you for killing your first mother. I am grateful that you killed your mother. If you had not killed your mother, I would not be able to marry Basilio. I am deeply grateful that you killed your mother.

Segismundo: Mother, don't be cruel! What do I need? I have nothing.

Gertrude: You need Oliver to do everything for you. I am needy too. Since I am needy for affection, I judge you by my lack of affection. If I say you are needy, even if you are not needy, you start becoming needy in the eyes of the public. And right now, you need me to get you out of the dungeon. You say: what are you doing for me, for my Puerto Rican cause? I do not say: what are you doing for me, for my American cause? If I do not lift a finger for you, you do not lift a finger. You expect something from me. I expect nothing from you.

Segismundo: Why don't you expect anything of me?

Gertrude: What can I expect from you? Can you provide for me like your father? Can you make good things happen? Must you always wait for the provider, the supplier? Do you think that you are special—that we owe you something—that we wronged you—that you are entitled—by needing us—by begging us to give you the *man-tengo*—the liberty—as if liberty were not something that you had to earn? Nobody ever gave me anything. I had to earn my position in life. I had to marry. Twice. You do not make it happen.

You depend on others to make it happen for you. And if they do not—you resent them— like you resent Oliver Exterminator and your father. That is why I am telling you—because I do not want you to resent me—because I own your liberty. I do not expect gratefulness not even from my son—beggar that he is—poorer in thanks than anybody. And cruel, like me, only to be kind. I never liked having a son. I saw Hamlet growing—and it did not make me any younger—it made me older. My son wants to take my place. To replace me. To make me old before my prime. When you have children they suck your time—your attention—the milk from your breasts. But do they nourish you? They give nothing. Everything is taking, expecting, little colonies of the western world. I would have pampered you, spoiled you—made you feel that you were the glass of fashion and the mould of affection. I would have given you so much food that you would be a fat prince. I would have given you a nanny—no contact with the populace. Your isolation would have been quite different—it would have had to do with excess—not with deprivation.

Segismundo: Excess and deprivation will meet at the end of this road in a place called hope. I have a mother and a father—you know what that means to me now—after years of being accused of killing my mother—I acquire by the grace of the muses—

a blonde mother—so beautiful she looks like a virgin. Such a loving mother—that I cry—crocodile tears—seven times salt. I would have liked to cry when I was a baby—when I lost my mother—when I had reasons to cry—but now I have reasons to celebrate my new bride-mother. There are two in front of me—a bride and a groom—and I form a triangle—no, not a triangle—there are not only three, there are four—a rectangle—a table for four. I have acquired a brother too—and I have always said: more is more—how can Fú be more than Fú and Fá.

Washy: *When two is one, one is half. I am not two wishing to be one. I am one for all and all for one. I am Statehood.*

Wishy: *I am Independence.*

Wishy-Washy: *I am a Colony, an Associated Free State. Like the clouds can be weasels, whales, and camels—I have three branches: to act, to do, and to perform. But I don't act the statehood. I don't do the independence. I perform the Wishy that washes the thought. And if you give me one face—Wishy—I'll give you another*

face—Washy. And I'll wipe
my face with both faces—
Wishy-Washy. And I'll have a
face for each day. If it is Wishy,
I'll wish my thoughts away
until the day turns over to the
dark side of the atmospheric,
meteorological coin—of life
versus morning rituals—and
night washes day away—and
swipes my desires.

Washy:

I am washing my thoughts
away. Sometimes it takes
longer than I think. Sometimes I am washing and I
wish I were wishing. Those
are conflicting times. I am
wishing and washing away
my thoughts at the same
time. But I have a contract
and in that contract it states
that I am only allowed to
Washy. Only Washy. But as I
started washing with all my
washing skills—I thought
I should not be washing
because if I wash it all out—
after washing and wash-
ing—there will be nothing

left to wash—but to wish that I were not washing.

Wishy-Washy: *That is why I never get tired of wishing and washing at the same time—and if I get tired of wishing I wash away my wishing as I wish away my washing. Why don't you become a Wishy-Washy instead of a Washy, Washy?*

Washy: *I would prefer not to. Even though I've washed all the dirty laundry, there are always more dirty dishes in the sink.*

Wishy-Washy: *If it pleases you to wish it— wish it—if it pleases you to wash it—wash it. Do as you please. Do as you wash when you wish. Do as you wish when you wash. The so-called minorities are majorities, but since less is more the more should feel that they are less. Why would you want me to believe that less is more unless you want to trick me and give me less money for my worth or my work? Unless more is not more less is more. And yes, minorities are more. They are majorities. But why call them minorities to minoritize their quantity and their quality—to make them feel that they are less when they are more. Why on earth would less be more unless you want to give more power to less and not to more— unless you want less to keep invading and pillaging the terrain and domain of more. That is why you invented the category of third world countries and first world countries because you wanted to say those third world countries are also minorities that are less because they are more. We are less, but we control the more, so more is less because less controls more. Less is more is a fabrication of the rich to make the poor think that by having less goodies they can have more babies. But less food for those babies. That is*

	what they mean when they say less is more. Less for you and more for me.
Washy:	*No.*
Wishy-Washy:	*You always say no.*
Washy:	*I say no to you, Wishy-Washy.*
Wishy:	*Wishy-Washy is not the only one wishing away your washing. I wish you were dead too.*
Wishy-Washy:	*Oh, Wishy, if you wish Washy were dead—what would become of you without Washy?*
Wishy:	*I would rule the world. Imagine all the people living for today. YA-HA-A-AA You may say I'm a dreamer. But I'm not the only one. I hope someday you'll join me. And the world will be as one.*

Hamlet: You can't kill Oliver. I'll kill him. You can't kill your father. I'll kill him. You can't kill Astolfo— oh, please, I'll kill him like I killed Laertes. I'll kill Oliver like I killed Polonius. I'll kill Basilio like I killed Claudius. I kill. Period. I act. I make your wishes come true. Didn't you say you wanted to kill them?

Segismundo: I didn't kill them.

Hamlet: I'll kill them.

Segismundo: You are horrible. Really, really horrible. Now I'll never get out of this fucking dungeon. Destructive. You're so destructive. Just because I said I want to—doesn't mean I will. Why would you want to kill my father? Can you tell me why? Why would you do that? I love my father. I just wanted to let him know that I suffer. The stars were right. Basilio's son would bring horrors to the state. Not I, but you, Hamlet. Why would you do that? Now I'll be damned forever. People will think I am a monster. I don't want to kill my father—it's you who wants to kill him. And you didn't kill your father. No. You come to my island to kill my father. You sick motherfucker.

Hamlet: Don't you see I'm here to help you?

Segismundo: Did I ask for your help?

Hamlet:	I feel for you. I've come to liberate you.
Segismundo:	Did I ask for your help?
Hamlet:	I heard you complaining about your lack of freedom. I said: what an unjust father. What is he doing—with his son in the dungeon of liberty—enclosed in a nutshell. I had to help you. I had to let you know that I care for you. That I thought your father was so unjust.
Segismundo:	No. You just go for the killing—to punish your mother for marrying my father. Why does it bother you? It doesn't bother me. In fact, the wedding party will liberate me from the dungeon. They're recognizing me as their son—as an heir to the throne. Why would it bother me that they're going to marry? And why does it bother you? You have such a loving mother—I can't tell you how much I admire her—she has come to visit me—and she has told me that soon I will be free. I owe it to the new feeling that is aroused in our two monarchs: love. My father is in love with your mother. And she asked him— as a wedding gift—for a presidential pardon— so I will be free. What you don't understand is that I might feel miserable—but I have never felt depressed. I am like a jack-in-the-box. The more you push me down—and your culture has really put me down—and accused me of things I have never done—like being a terrorist—how

can I be a terrorist if I have never been given a chance to exist? Maybe if I had that chance I would have the ability and desire to question: to be or not to be. But right now that question is out of the question. I have to be what I am: a jack-in-the-box. The more you push me down—and you have really pushed me down—to consider me a nonentity, an alien, when I exist, I breathe. And, like a jack-in-the-box, I jump back up and say: but I always love life!

I don't divide and conquer. I conquer without having to divide. Because I am complete. And you are half and half—always wanting to cut in half. And the more you see completeness—the more you cut into incompleteness, fragmentation, a mess of a being. You cut me in half—you cut me in half—and no matter how much you damage—there is no damage control. You keep reducing the scope of the other—to make me less—and no more. To make me doubt myself. To not let me grow. And if I grow—it is certainly not because you want me to grow. On the contrary. You want me to become less and less—until I become dust—and you cough. And then you say:

> —*You're causing trouble. You made me cough. If I get sick I will sue you. And my father who art in heaven will invade you.*

The method of your madness is not my method. You were born on the top—and you fell into the pit of Ground Zero. I was born to raise hell as the voice of the dungeon. Nobody expected anything of me—nothing. And that is when the unexpected unfolds its wisdom against all the expectations that amounted to zero to the bone. Stop creating hard labor for my people—labor that doesn't develop their higher standard of expectation—only your method of extermination. There is no doubt in my mind that Oliver Exterminator is a descendant of your race of exterminators—through race and sex—only race and sex—in all the tabloids—the only thing that counts is race and sex—maybe because these are topics that you can control—and with them exterminate with a spray of raid. Everything is a raid of extermination. Destruction. Not creation. And you don't love either. You don't nourish the entrails. You disembody the bowels. You create havoc. And you kill. I create what you later destroy. You are always at the end. But I am always at the beginning. Starting. You say you are a higher man, but you are a lower man—because your standard of expectation is low—you expect nothing of people like me—you put us on welfare—in confinement—on hold. In the meantime you take what you can catch—destiny, fame, history, politics, civilization, and you kill—attention getter—always playing the main role—even when you have nothing to say—or even when you drop dead center stage—nobody can take you out—you steal the attention of the rest of the world—with your havoc—with your pestering methods of bulldozing the grass—until there is nothing left—the rest is silence.

[The presidential suite at the Waldorf Astoria.]

Gertrude: *A las burbujas de la vida*, Basilio.

Basilio: Gertrude, who taught you Spanish?

Gertrude: *La Española Inglesa.* Oh, I am getting drunk.
              I have this little habit of drinking champagne.
              Basilio, my son likes to crack nuts, he likes
              nuts—that is why he walks with Zarathustra
              and Giannina. And he likes riddles and puz-
              zles—but always to crack them wide open—
              and make noise when he cracks them open. I,
              on the other hand, like bubbles in the sand—
              those bubbles of champagne. I cannot read cof-
              fee grains like the Greeks, but I read the bubbles
              of champagne and the bubbles of the sea.

Basilio: Oh, Gertrude, Gertrude, I am ugly, Catholic,
              and sentimental. And superstitious too.

Gertrude: Oh, if only I had done what you did. The horo-
              scope said Hamlet would bring horrors to the
              state. But I did not take preventive medicine. I
              should have imprisoned my son in the dungeon
              of liberty like you did.

Basilio: You did not see a reason to do it. My wife died
              the day Segismundo was born.

Gertrude: And God was sick the day Hamlet was born.

Basilio:

> But your husband did not die the day he was born. Do not blame yourself, Gertrude. We have a lot to learn from each other. *Tanto monta, monta tanto Gertrude como Basilio.*

Gertrude:

> The sun will never set on our empire. We shall melt the sun with our global warming. Our colonies shall direct our purposes.

Basilio:

> Better to keep the puppies of war on a leash—howling—their feelings—they are only allowed to express their feelings—even if they are too emotional—for my taste—not of noble blood, rather of the rabble—princes and prisoners of the state, both our dear, dear sons, Hamlet and Segismundo: the best of both worlds:
>
> > *Pan, tierra y libertad: Salud!*
> > *Inclitas Razas Ubérrimas!*
> > *Sangre de Hispania Fecunda!*
> > *Salve!*

Gertrude:

I can claim Segismundo as my new immigrant—the model for illegal extraterrestrial aliens who arrive without a passport or a green card. He is making the case for the voiceless. I take pride in him as a product of my culture. Look how we have messed up the world—but we still created a great guy even if he is a fucked-up little bastard. We will give him the legitimacy you never gave him. We will love Puerto Rico. And we realize how important it will be for us—even for you—Basilio—when we marry—to make Segismundo a state—the empire will not collapse—through the prophesy that the U. S. of B. will split into multiple independent states—and that the first one to secede from the empire will be Segismundo's island of bananas—Puerto Rico. To stop the prophesy from becoming true—not only do we have to marry—the day we marry we will make Puerto Rico a state. Then will come Argentina, Haiti, Brazil, Venezuela, Colombia, Aibonito, Naranjito, Isla Verde—all of them—instead of seceding—will come to us—to our empire. Let us keep our focus on Puerto Rico. We must show the world that we love what is ours—not that we neglect our own. If others see that we love Puerto Rico—and also Puerto Rico sees that we love Puerto Rico—they will want us more.

[The United States of Banana has decided that, regardless of Puerto Rico's vote to become independent or to become a state, the United States has declared Puerto Rico a state of exception, a state of emergence, an emergent state.]

Gertrude: And this I say without caring a hoot about the decision that the island makes or does not make. The people have had enough time to decide—and they did not. Now we have to make the tough decision for them—as a gift. We God giving people give God-given gifts—as wedding gifts. We will grant not only a poetic license to Segismundo to attend our wedding—we will grant statehood to the island of Puerto Rico. Imperative—to prove that we are not racists—that we want Puerto Rico to be the first Latin American country to become a state of the union. Then will come Mexico, Nicaragua, Suriname, Costa Rica, Ecuador, Santo Domingo, Martinique…

[At the United Nations, they are discussing Cuba's invasion of Puerto Rico. Both Cuba and the United States of Banana are claiming sovereignty over Puerto Rico.]

Cuba: We are willing to negotiate everything—except sovereignty, equality, and the right to self-determination. We are willing to discuss everything, human rights, freedom of press, political prisoners, everything they want to talk about, but as equals, without the slightest shadow cast on our sovereignty, and without the slightest violation of the Cuban people's right to self-determination.

Argentina: We have been laughing all along at Puerto Rico's lack of dignity. Puerto Rico doesn't know what it wants. Puerto Rico is neither Fú nor Fá. It's a little snot in the world—an ah-choo—a fart in the universe. Whoever thought that to become what we already are—Americans—we have to become Puerto Ricans.

Cuba: *No son ni Fú ni Fá*. And that is what the U. S. of B. is offering us—to become like Puerto Ricans—*ni Fú ni Fá*. A captive island. I am la Mayor de las Antillas Mayores. I am one wing of the bird, el Caribe. I need my other wing to fly. The U. S. of B. does not need the wing of Puerto Rico to fly. The U. S. of B. uses the wing of Puerto Rico as a feather in its cap—it has rendered its wing useless. We, Cubans, claim sovereignty over Puerto Rico. We want Puerto

Rico to feel useful—to have a sense of trajec-tory—of route—to know where it is going—not to belly-crawl like a reptile through the desert trenches of Iraq and Afghanistan—but to soar with Cuba at its side—to fly away from the U. S. of B.—to free its wing that is dead pinned to the bald eagle that renders its little wing useless.

U. S. of B.:   Puerto Rico has asked for our intervention. Cuba has invaded Puerto Rico.

Cuba: We hereby proclaim that the wing of Puerto Rico is a feather that has a history that must be writ-ten with ink in Spanish. We have come to liber-ate Puerto Rico from the atrocity of having lost its way, of being confused, of not knowing who it is or what it wants. It claims to be Wishy-Washy. *Los puertorriqueños no son ni Fú ni Fá*. We will make them strong. We will take care of our little sister. We will protect her shores. No more Americans. No more English nor Spanglish—excuses of colo-nialism—to confuse the identity of Puerto Rico, which is clearly Spanish—an island—the wing of a bird—el Caribe—and its other wing is Cuba. If Cuba and Puerto Rico are two wings of the same bird—why aren't those two wings flying? Because Cuba and Puerto Rico are not talking. That's why neither Cuba nor Puerto Rico is able to fly. Why? Because Puerto Rico is one wing of a bird that has two wings—and the other wing is Cuba—and those two wings don't belong to the same bird anymore. They are attached to bodies that don't fit. Imagine a pitirre's wing attached with a safety pin to an eagle's chest. Of course, the eagle says:

> —*Your wing is too small. It won't help me hunt for moles and rats.*

But why is a pitirre lending its wing to an eagle that doesn't understand its songs or its diet of seeds and nuts. Why should it sing with a dead beast in its stomach or attack with weapons of mass destruction, mechanical birds, languages foreign to the constitution of its pitirre's beak? No wonder the eagle calls the pitirre a welfare state—and talks about its dysfunction—because it has plucked its fragile petite wing out of context. It has misused its function—and now it says that it doesn't work. But I know that wing will work if you give it back to the bird to which it belongs. I know that bird will start singing the best songs it has ever sung as soon as it regains its function. Let it find its wings—let it be what it is—a bird—with two wings. Let it spread its wings and fly.

Puerto Rico:

But I also love to ride on top of the bald eagle, spread my little wing and sing on top of that eagle, sing a song that inspires that eagle, that makes him stop and think:

> —*Where is this music coming from?*

From a bird that has only one wing—that misses its other wing. Its inspiration comes from its missing wing. But it is happy when it soars on top of the eagle and spreads its only wing and sings.

U. S. of B.: Puerto Rico does not want to be Cuban. Puerto Rico wants to be American.

Puerto Rico: I don't know what I want.

Cuba: You want what I have. You have no choice to become anything but Cuban.

Puerto Rico: Why do I have to become Cuban if I am already Puerto Rican?

Cuba: Puerto Rico must belong to Cuba in order to become *Cuba libre.* By becoming Cuban, Puerto Rico will find its lost identity, the identity it lost when it became American.

U. S. of B.: The first step to becoming Puerto Rican is accepting our passport. But if you accept our passport—you must give us something in return. Don't you want to become Americans?

Argentina & Cuba: We are already Americans. It's redundant. We will accept your passport as reparations for what you have taken from us. But we will not forfeit our Argentine and Cuban passports.

U. S. of B.:	So you want to be Puerto Rican? Have an American passport—and continue being Argentine and Cuban.
Argentina & Cuba:	No, no, no—we'll take your passport—but keep our sovereignty.
U. S. of B.:	Is that what it takes? Puerto Rico, do you want to have a Puerto Rican passport to be like Cuba and Argentina?
Puerto Rico:	Yes, we do.
U. S. of B.:	Granted. You will have your Puerto Rican passport.
Puerto Rico:	And we want our coins, our self-determination, sovereignty coins.
U. S. of B.:	Grant them that, also. What else do you want?
Puerto Rico:	Our independence.

[Watching the news on TV.]

Giannina: It was all worked out by Gertrude and Basilio. They lifted the embargo on Cuba with the condition that the Gusanos could go back to Cuba, but the Gusanos went back to Cuba with an imperialistic mission—as agents of Gertrude and Basilio—to infiltrate and convince the Cuban people that they should be the United States of el Caribe—that all islands of the Antillas Mayores should become Cuban because Cuba is the largest island of the Antillas Mayores and the favorite of the Spanish Empire. So, they invaded Puerto Rico in the name of *la madre patria, España,* and proclaimed that Puerto Ricans were no longer Puerto Ricans but Cubans. It was a clever idea—if only they had unified the islands in the name of el Caribe—but it was not el Caribe that they were all becoming—it was Cubans—smaller than what they were already and losing their own identities. Only later was it discovered that it was all a plot by Gertrude and Basilio—who sent the Gusanos to Cuba to invade Puerto Rico—so they would have the perfect excuse to invade Cuba—which is what they wanted to do from the beginning. They were afraid the Russians would return to Cuba—because the Americans were using Poland to aim missiles supposedly at Iran, Iraq, and Afghanistan—but they were really directed at Russia. Puerto Rico was just an excuse. The target was Cuba.

Hamlet: It was Cuba's fault for invading Puerto Rico.

Giannina: But don't you see that the Cuban invasion of Puerto Rico was provoked by the U. S. of B.?

Hamlet: How?

Giannina: They wanted Cuba. They lifted the embargo and sent the Gusanos back home with the imperialistic notion that Cuba should be the leader of el Caribe. In reality Gertrude and Basilio didn't want the integrity of el Caribe. What they wanted was war in el Caribe. They wanted to divide and conquer. So they incited Cuba to invade Puerto Rico. And when Cuba invaded Puerto Rico, then they invaded Cuba for having invaded Puerto Rico.

[Still in his cell.]

Segismundo: For a very long time I was told by the doctors of
the Royal Academy who came to the dungeon
to examine my body and my brain that I come
from a race of lazy, brutal happy-go-luckies—
that the best I could do in life was to depend
upon a wealthy empire to support me—because
I couldn't earn my daily bread in any other
way—because I lacked advancement—and for a
very long time I believed that I lacked advancement—and when I spoke Spanish, Spanglish,
or English—I stuttered—and I tried to enter
the grammatical system of the doctors of the
Royal Academy who examined my tongue to
see if I was a stuttering dyslexic, or if I had an
attention deficit spam—because I couldn't capture knowledge and pictures and plots the way
normal and clever people do. They called me an
idiot savant who is taught but doesn't learn—
the logic of destruction—it works in construction—it demolishes buildings of civilizations
that are much more advanced than the logic of
destruction—it demolishes our free thinking—
and our economic progress—to make us depend
on a system of demolition, of waste, of deprivation, of demoralization. Do you know what
it is that everything you construct with love is
demolished by a wrecking ball that imposes its
inflexibility of cleverness and smartness, and air
conditions and radios, and computers deleting

your constructions? Because there was always a problem inside my constructions. The problem, in itself, was my creativity. That I gave birth to eggs—that eggs were laid—without blood—that I was not a pregnant woman—but a chicken, a hen. That my chickens were hatched with their heads on. That their heads had to be cut off. There was always a problem with my creativity—and the crane always came to demolish the problem—but when it demolished the problem—it demolished my way of thinking—because it was not the American way of thinking—the American way of life—the correct way of doing things—the practical way. There was always a problem—and my problem was that I let the academics demolish my structures—that I thought my thoughts could possibly get better if I entered the system of demolition—if I let them have a say in my work—if I let them destroy me—I could construct myself again—because I always reconstruct myself—because I loved constructions—because I was an architect—because I was naïve—and I believed I had a life ahead of me—but the life that I had ahead of me became the life that was behind me—all of a sudden I am 50 years old—and I see the system of demolition—of radical demolition in my work—it has taken away—it has not finished the thought of demolition—it is not complete—it comes with arrogance—the crane of the smart and clever—and it demolishes my thought structures—and it says—*this is wrong and this is wrong and this is wrong and what is right is because it is wrong*—it is always like that—in my experience it has always been like that—that what is wrong is wrong because it is right. Once came a stupid man to tell me—you are wrong. I believed him because he spoke with authority. I kept my thought to myself—but I thought— maybe I am wrong. Why not? I don't need the stupid man to tell me I am wrong. I have always doubted myself first. He just confirmed my suspicions. But I thought—there is something right here. I will take the wrong out of the right. I will know what is right and what is wrong. So I asked another man: what is wrong here? And he answered—what is wrong here is that you are right. And I asked myself—am I righteous. Because when I am wrong I am right. How did I develop my good luck in life? First, I found out Oliver had bad luck. Then I figured out where his bad luck came from. It came from denying all that I thought was right. He said no, no, no all the time. And I thought I deserved yes, yes, yes. So the more rights he denied me, the more rights I granted myself—even though he cast shadows on my thoughts—that make me think I am wrong when I am right. I overcome these shadows and assert my rights as lucky strikes.

I don't believe the new is better than the old or the old better than the new—but I affirm my way of doing the world all over again—the way my hands mold it and my ears hear the tides break—and my knowledge—through the accumulation of experience—acquires a different perception—than a representation of reality. The representation of reality is an obstacle to the advancement of knowledge, and so is all the literature of entertainment that is impeding the advancement of thought and the blowing of minds. We have to leap over all these obstacles—furniture of entertainment—distractions and dispersions—we have to center ourselves in the third eye—and liquidate the office cubicle— fire the boss of outdated control techniques— plots of introductions without a messy substance. There is nothing inside a memo—nothing inside an ID—nothing inside a computer. Strategic planning is not planning our future ahead of our time—but bossing our energy around—until we feel we can't move, we can't take a vacation, we can't have any fun without the superpower structure threatening to crush our bones. And what about dictionaries—the meaning of manners, the modes of definition, the ways in which we say what has been said a million times are rooted in false premises. We should pull up the roots—so we can see how small or how big they really are—and denounce their authority—deflate their pressure in our lives—the pressure for money's sake—practicality—and what we call our choices have already been chosen by others—to suit the costumes of a fleeting moment that sways in the fragile air we breathe. There is no motion that has not been strangled into ways of thinking—and the ways are wrong—they are based on preconceptions of the information age. Information is not ahead of our time. Information is the beginning of analphabetism. The meaning of things is found in the thing itself. Your eye in contact with the shape of the thing finds a contact—and you can establish a relationship with that thing—this relationship is not found in any dictionary—it has no origin—only the origin of settlement—where I settle some of my affairs—others are never settled—but they lay upon that settlement a bunch of eggs.

With your policy of divide and conquer you can no longer conquer what you divided. In fact, you never conquered what you divided. If you had conquered it—it would still be with you—but you never conquered it—what you did was divide it. And the divisions of races—of religions—of sects—between people who have more in common with themselves than with you—are coming back to haunt you—they are the dead bodies that you carry on your back.

There is a higher standard of expectation, and there is a higher standard of living, and I always thought that a higher standard of living promoted a higher standard of expectation. But I was a fool—and I was naïve—and I thought that you would expect the best of me—but the best was always the best for your idea of empire—not for my sovereignty. I have to divorce my higher standard of expectation from my higher standard of living because my higher standard of living is not living up to my higher standard of expectation. You control my standard of expectation through my standard of living. Giving me food and cleaning my clothes you make me depend on your priorities. I hold my higher standard of expectation higher than your higher standard of living. Your standard of living is your higher standard of expectation. But your expectations of me have lowered my standards—and I have to separate myself from your expectations—so that I can claim the liberty to be free from an associated state. The freedom that I will claim is an interior freedom, but that freedom, which I have inhabited for a very long time, will blow Puerto Rico's mind out of the association that has harmed its sovereignty.

I have not accepted success until now—and I could have—because success is not a one-way street—and once you think you are there you think you made it forever. And there is no forever in success. You succeed—and then you have to start from scratch again—and become that thing that all of you listening to me here fear—the fear of the unknown—and what can happen—when your foundation is taken out from under you—and either you learn to jump in the air—without foundation—and that's the success—the success of jubilation—in the fragmentation. Even though I have been cut all over—I am full of cuts—and I bleed all over—those are my editors who cut me—to take away my impurities—but with all my cuts bleeding and fragmentations—I will not stop jumping in the air—without foundation—until I reach the top of the ceiling and I break through it by jumping in the air without foundations—and I have foundations—but my foundations have taught me that the best foundations are found when there is no foundation—but there's a there, there—there's a being in that foundation that is breaking the air, the tidal wave and the hair.

[The general assembly of the United Nations of Banana moves to the crown of the Statue of Liberty to celebrate the wedding of the century.]

Gertrude & Basilio (*speaking in unison*): We are here gathered tonight to celebrate our wedding, the marriage of the north and the south, the marriage of Spanish and English, the marriage of Hamlet and Segismundo. And we have taken Segismundo out of the dungeon. We are making Puerto Rico the 51st state of the U. S. of Banana. Segismundo, the soul mate of Hamlet, he has missed his brother for all that it has lasted his confinement—and out of a miraculous lightness of being—a political license has been granted. We pardon this prisoner—who killed his mother— when he was born.

Segismundo (*aside*): Mother, I never meant to kill you. Don't take me wrong. These politicians do everything for more votes. Their higher standard of living will be opposed by my higher standard of expectation.

Basilio: The stars were wrong—they made obvious to me that Segismundo would be an enemy of the state—the way Hamlet turned out to be to the state of Denmark—and I used my magic power—preventive medicine. It won't happen to me—I won't pamper my son—I will not do what my beautiful bride (like a virgin) did. I did what I had to do—raise myself and my people—and leave my son out of the picture.

The stars had said—he would be a horror to the state—and the people of Puerto Rico had already proved that they are *macheteros* and terrorists—so I put him on hold—I checked on him every day—I knew that one day I would elevate him to the crown. The occasion is now. Now is the moment when Gertrude and Basilio will be crowned king and queen of the Americas—and our sons—Hamlet and Segismundo—will be here—to witness our accomplishments as gratifications of our purposes. Segismundo, as a gift to your mother—Gertrude—who implored me to give you a second chance—and a second wing—I have brought you to the crown—to meet your soul mate—another great poet—like you—off the edge—like you—with a skewed sense of reality—like you—to meet your match—as we market this wedding as the wedding of the century—and one of the greatest accomplishments on this planet. With our wedding we will unite the north and south—the two child prodigies—and the two prodigal sons—under parental supervision. And as a wedding gift to my lovebird, Gertrude, we will not only pardon Segismundo but make Puerto Rico a state. Not only is Segismundo in the crown—after being in the dungeon—but all the citizens of Puerto Rico will no longer be second-class citizens but first-class—crown, crown, crown. And crown that cockles—hen. I upgraded their status—they no longer will fly *en la guagua aérea* as tourists—but as first-class passengers. And as the third and last gift to my lovebird (like a virgin) queen what Puerto Rico was—Latin America will be. I will grant—as the other prodigy to my dear birdy—Gertie—the possibility for all Latin American citizens to cross the borders *como Pedro por su casa.* This is America, the beautiful. A green card, and if you please, a passport, an American passport, for all Latin Americans—to cross the borders and make a living in dream, dream, dream—the land of the Statue of Liberty—under whose crown we are celebrating this gala to make Puerto Rico a state and to make all Latin American citizens American citizens.

Segismundo: I want to live in America.

Basilio: Puerto Rico, you are already a state, and Segismundo, you are free.

Segismundo: I want to be free from freedom. Free. And in another state of mind that doesn't promote Imperial France.

Hamlet: This is not Imperial France. This is America, the beautiful.

Basilio: And to start our rendezvous let me present my bride to our sons Hamlet and Segismundo.

Gertrude:	Segismundo, prince of Poland who speaks Spanish.

Hamlet:	Oh, the bitch who bore me is again in heat!

Basilio:	Hamlet, prince of Denmark, speaking English.

Hamlet (*looking at Segismundo with suspicion*): We hardly know each other, but we do know each other. We have been talking to each other for centuries. Our poetry is the poetry of the children of this planet.

Segismundo:	Hamlet, this is my father, the great Basilio, King of Poland, speaking Spanish, *a sus órdenes.*

Hamlet:	And this is the bitch who bore me again and again in heat—this bitch is always ovulating—Gertrude (like a virgin), queen, and always will be Queen of Denmark, speaking English, like a Brit. Come, Segismundo, our acquaintances are here. Let's talk to Rosencrantz and Guildenstern.

Segismundo:	No, wait, I can't let the proclamations pass without my response. My silence will be cursed. And all those academic sharks are waiting to catch me in the mouthtrap and say: Gotcha! Not this time, sharks, academic sharks, I am in top shape—and I will not be caught like a common fish with your bait. (*Segismundo, center stage, looking into the spotlight.*) It figures. All

this, it figures. You can figure all these decompositions and compositions as bodies that are disembodied—that no longer find themselves at ease in their bodies—and are looking for other answers—to answer their calls—but they walk like chickens with their heads cut off. As my dear, dear father, who was so good to me since I was born that he forgave me the unusual sin of killing my mother the day I was born, has granted me through the graces of the muses another loving mother who pardons the sin of her stepchild—of course, it's in their self-interest and the interests of their higher standard of living to pardon me—and to liberate me and my people from the dungeon and to upgrade our American citizenship—these selfless creatures who grant us so much good nature and generosity of spirit pouring through their global warming hearts—and their political ambition is nothing but noble to their higher standard of living—but adding a complement to a disjunction—it lowers my standard of expectation and that of my people to become a state. And as they proclaim *(de boca para afuera nada más)* the statehood of Puerto Rico I proclaim, as the Prince of the Gutter—the independence of Puerto Rico from the U. S. of Banana—and its adherence to Cuba—as the second wing of that bird that has two wings to fly—el Caribe—and not el Hilton. I challenge my father to a duel—after the coronation, the wedding and the party—but first the party, the drunken blast, the blurry flurry of recognition, the anagnorisis—of where I am—and of who these people are—and the enjoyment—all Puerto Rican and Latin American citizens—and their representatives in this gala are crazy to have a jolly good time—after the night—we'll end *con los rosarios de la aurora*—and we'll pick a bone—to fight—statehood—Basilio—independence—Segismundo—Washy, Wishy, and the world will be as one. It bites and itches from how ugly and rotten it is.

Statue of Liberty (*speaking through a loudspeaker*): I am speechless. He is fulfilling his promise to his people. I am speechless—soon—my genie—soon. I will leave—when he leaves—somebody—or myself— I might have to do it myself—self-reliance. I can't depend on anybody—these days—everybody is on his own—attending to his own profits and subjects. I'll have to uncork my own torch—get blasted and drunk. I have been waiting—and waiting—all these years as a frigid statue— soon—my genie—not soon enough—this dawn—when the cock crows—*cuando vengan los rosarios de la aurora*—when the cocks fight and kick their spurs—my genie—uncorked—free from freedom. Free. My genie uncorked. And I will ride away on the back of his horse—wherever his spurs lead me. Free from freedom. Free.

Basilio: But I am offering you my best: statehood.

Segismundo: The best of yourself is not statehood. It's liberty. Lady Liberty up there will sing tonight when the fat lady sings. It is always like this, Father, self-interest, created interest, corporate interest, and gas prices—stop our growth, to prevent our higher standards of expectations from manifesting themselves. Not this time, Daddy Yankee. The stars are on my side.

[The performers go first. Giannina, up front.]

Giannina:

Since the stars are on your side and me too. Let me sing to you this poem of the fortune-teller:

> *I have been a fortune-teller. Ages ago, I told the fortune of buffoons and mad-men. You remember. I had a small voice like a grain of sand and enormous hands. Madmen walked over my hands. I told them the truth. I could never lie to them. And now I am sorry. Ages ago, a drunk-ard filled with dreams asked me to dance. I used my cards to tell his fortune when his drinks became blows. My banging on the door killed the sea. Memories finished us. Madmen and buffoons count the grains of sand and have never destroyed night's dreams. They draw up the night and rise filled with middays. Magicians were and always will be my companions. Without guessing their tricks I started fire in their throats. But none explode. Maybe one. And with the fish another chimera rises.*

Let me propose a toast. To Hamlet and Segismundo: the best of both worlds. And with this glass of champagne—I propose a toast to *divina locura*—divine madness that has always inspired the higher expectations of the great poets throughout the globe. And I propose raising to this magnificent crown—divine madness that, like the oppressed everywhere, has been kept down—in submission, in seclusion, deprivation, and silence—and has been kept down by the antithesis of divine madness, divine expectation, divine philosophy, and poetry—by the enemies of greatness and the lovers of entertainment who have spit in the eyes and slapped the cheeks of poetry and philosophy—with the cheapening of the heart—the cheapening of all that is high and noble—the cheapening of all the greatness, the magnificence, the beauty, the good, the noble, the suspension of the senses, the charisma, and the good energy that spells through our good will—something good for America—something that makes America rise again from the tippy-top of the Yukon, to the tippy-toe of la Tierra del Fuego, and that is Segismundo, *mi amor*, hic. I have hiccups again.

> *I love hiccups and I love sneezes and I*
> *love blinks and I love belches and I love*
> *gluttons. I love hair. I love bears. For me*
> *the round. For me the world. Round is*
> *the happy face. And round is the midday.*
> *And when the moon is most beautiful is*
> *when its round. Sex is round. And the*
> *heart also. The hand is round. The mouth*
> *also. Sneezes are round. And hiccups*
> *also. When they appear the graces are*

> *on my side. And the skies are clear, to fly,*
> *birdy, fly.*

Hamlet:

You are not supposed to spill the beans of goodness.

Giannina:

I know, my advisers told me I should be specific. But I don't pay attention to what the media wants—to catch me off guard. Goodness is goodness.

Hamlet:

What do you mean by something good for America?

Giannina:

What do I mean? Goodness is goodness, that's what I mean, something high, something admirable, something noble, of the nobility of the spirit, the best of both worlds, that's what I mean, I wish the best. We should not define or specify what is the best for us because what we consider the best might not be the best for us. That's why my wishes always come true. I make them real. I make them the best. (*Looking around, she catches sight of a man—in the corner.*) I can't believe my eyes, Rubén Darío—wishing for the best, the noble, the good, I catch a glimpse of you, the originator of this renaissance in America. It was you—Darío—*el mestizo*—my soul mate, *mi amor*—who said.

Rubén Darío & Giannina (*in unison*): Hamlet and Segismundo: the best of both worlds:

> *If Segismundo grieves,*
> *Hamlet feels it.*

Giannina:

I can't believe my eyes. Peter Pan of Latin America. You stole the French meters at that time and you brought their abundance and richness to Spain and Latin America.

Rubén Darío:

You mean Robin Hood?

Giannina:

I do the same—steal from the rich to give to the poor. But who is the poor? I give also to the poor who are the rich living in misery—because their higher standards of living don't match their lower standards of expectation. When there exists so much poverty of spirit, misery—cheapening of our souls—how can you create great poetry? Anyway, I am so glad to see you, *mi anagnorisis*, my love. With us—with you and me—Darío and Braschi—things start to shake up—and beans are spilled—let also the champagne spill—we are tacky—our strength is also in the tacky—but in the philosophical love of humanity. Let's break a glass of champagne. In our good names.

> *Pan, tierra y libertad.*
> *Salud.*

Sangre de Hispania fecunda.
Inclitas Razas Ubérrimas.

More champagne, please. For him and me,
together, forever again. And these, Rubén
Darío, are my companions on this long voyage.
Hamlet, you already know—the poet actor.

Rubén Darío:

Hamlet, he is the spitting image of Antonin
Artaud.

Giannina:

Both are mad—mad as the sea and wind when
both contend which is the mightier. Hamlet or
Antonin Artaud.

Antonin Artaud:

The actor is an athlete of the heart.

Giannina:

And so is the poet—an athlete of the heart.

Antonin Artaud:

I am playing the role of Hamlet. I only have one
possibility—to go backwards in time—in memory—but now I have broken the spell of always
living in the straitjacket of memory—walking
backwards like a crab—if like a crab I could go
back in memory. Now I am exercising all the
muscles of my body with your theory of the
poet actor.

Giannina:

Thank you. Rubén Darío, here is also the poet
philosopher. The master of my ship, the captain
of my soul, Zarathustra, *mi amor.*

Zarathustra: Where's the overman? I came here to meet him.
And I only see poets—no, please, adulators,
vanity, poets of the sea, who don't know who
they are. Whenever you give a compliment,
Giannina, you always say thank you. And you
ignore that the other person has not returned
your compliment with another compliment. You
are so insecure that you're always giving compliments—expecting them back—and you give the
gratitude—before it comes back. You say:

—You have a beautiful voice.

You wait a minute. The person you compli-
mented doesn't return your call for another
compliment. But in your mind you already
received it—and you say:

—Thank you.

Giannina: Thank you. Thank you, very much (*applause*).
Thank you (*applause*). Thank you. I drink
goat's milk—and I laugh like a goat and jump
like a rabbit. I don't even know if I am floating
in the air—I certainly have no floor under my
feet—so how is it that I can stand still and look
at you—and say these things. And I have here
my two goblins with me. Let me introduce
them to you—Antonin Artaud—and to you—
Rubén Darío. This is Charmides. And this is
Laches.

Rubén Darío:	Laches means *leche* in Spanish.
Giannina:	And Charmides means charm in Greek. And it also means karma, destiny. Both of them are dressed in white suits—and they are goblins— not ghosts.
Hamlet:	Bad conscience is cruelty walking backwards.
Artaud:	Cruelty is a charm.
Giannina:	No, a grace. I don't know how to say it, but I was initiated into the mysteries by Socrates. It was Zarathustra, my anagnorisis, *mi amor*, the captain of my ship, the owner of my soul, who wrote a letter to Socrates asking him if I could continue my studies with him—after having studied with Zarathustra for years.

Socrates:	*She is too old. She already lost her period.*
Zarathustra:	*She is ready. I guarantee you that. Having followed the ascetic ideals of chastity, humility, poverty. She never married, never acquired wealth—and being simple, not clever but simple—she is as ready as a thirteen-year-old boy like Theaete-*

tus—maybe less—maybe nine—look at her cheeks— rosy—innocent—joyful.   I rid her of the disgust that was fuming and foaming around her mouth like a crust—I rid it by affirming the being of life—as it is—in the moment it comes to be as it is—the experience of a child in labor with another child—swaddling her in pampers—so that youth returns—like an incantation—fresh, divine— through rituals of fire, water, air, earth.

Basilio: I am versed in the occult. I have a collection of telescopes and astrolobes acquired through the hands of an antique collector named Elli Buk. I am also a reader of theater. My favorites are Witkiewicz and Kantor.

Hamlet: *The Mother* is my mother Gertrude. And *The Madman and the Nun* are Ophelia and me.

Giannina: Put the donkey first so it won't get spooked. The quality of my life is rising to a very high pitch of a musical score already written—and I play the score with my ten fingers—but in reality the players of the piano are Laches and

Charmides, milk and charm, the goblins of the poet child—who is always playing hide and seek—and at my age he comes and goes—and he is hard to find. I never find him—I look for him everywhere—but I never find him—it is he who comes to me—who reveals himself to me—crying—for me to change his diapers. I am not his mother—but his shit is a sign of good luck.

Zarathustra: Which one is *el niño de teta*?

Giannina: Theaetetus, the nine-year-old boy who is always sucking the tit of the motley cow.

Zarathustra: Well, *teta*, Theaetetus, *niño de teta*, with charm and milk—make a good combo—inspiration and commotion with motion, dynamism—and wings—but not the wings—but a multitude of whirrs, trails, bouquets, roses, umbrellas, and fountains.

Giannina: This poet child has many faces—no—many smiles—they are all hidden—his smiles— behind his baby teeth that shine like sapphires in the mud. Usually, I lose one of my diamond studs, or one of my baby teeth, or one of my gloves. When I lose them—it is disconcerting—there is no concert—and no music—and if there is an agreement in the elements—these

elements agree to disagree—they are disagree-
able elements—and they make me lose a baby
tooth, a baby diamond, a white glove. Only
one of the pair is missing—one of the baby
diamonds, one of the gloves, one of the baby
teeth—but how can I bite if I am missing one of
the pair. And it is a winter day—and I need my
other white glove—my fingernails are blue like
the Indian summer on a winter afternoon. With
garlands on my head Socrates initiated me into
the mysteries of life and death. I was all dressed
in white—in a long white gown or tunic—not of
silk—but of cotton—wrinkled cotton—he took
me to the waters of lilies—they were very cold—
those waters—and I am not accustomed to cold
waters—but to lukewarm waters—the waters
of Wishy-Washy. Frogs drown in lukewarm
waters—cold waters awaken frogs—and so do
hot waters—but in lukewarm waters frogs like
Puerto Ricans drown cozy—watching a movie
on TV—and eating hamburgers and french
fries—cushy—cushy—cushions—in lukewarm
waters they drown: Puerto Ricans and frogs—
they drown. He was teaching me the mysteries
of lilies—and he said:

> —*Don't you want to become un niño de
> teta, like Theatetus, so that I can take you
> as one of my disciples?*

I need a lover—that's what I need. A lover who introduces me to the mysteries of the occult.

Zarathustra: Socrates will take care of that. And if not him, he will send you to Diotima. Do you know that Diotima stopped the plague from entering her city for more than ten years?

Giannina: A plague can be stopped? Well, maybe she can stop the plagues that will come unless Segismundo is freed from the dungeon.

Gertrude:	And we'll be great forever again! We'll marry Hamlet and Giannina, and Segismundo and Ophelia. To breed for us again! The stock of the populace—Segismundo who has been nurtured by the rabble of terrorists and beggars and bumps in the dungeon—and who has the pulse of the people—will marry an aristocrat—Ophelia—a blue blood in need of new blood—red and healthy—to energize our monarchy.
Basilio:	It will be good for them too!
Gertrude:	Of course, it will be good! Renovation, restoration, change. The stakes are running high! Will Hamlet give up Ophelia?
Basilio:	Gladly! But will Segismundo want her?
Gertrude:	Basilio, let me introduce you to Ophelia—my son's mistress. She will marry Segismundo.
Ophelia:	*To a nunnery*—he said—*get thee to a nunnery.* And I went mad.
Giannina:	I was also sent to a nunnery—by my father—but I didn't obey. I will fight the establishment against the father in favor of the son. I'll join the revolution on the side of Segismundo.
Hamlet:	Why is it—can you explain it to me—that some women nourish your weakness and others

nourish your strength? With Giannina I throw my shoulders back and walk straight like a stick, but when Ophelia approaches—I crawl into my mother's lap—no good, no good for my soul—and no good for hers.

Segismundo: I feel for Ophelia—poor gringa weakling. She looks like a Chinese dumpling. I could eat her up with chopsticks. I could break her bones with my teeth. Although her blood is blue, I see red blood running through her blue veins. I feel no pity for Ophelia. Enough of poor little rat! No time—you hear this, Hamlet—no time for miseries and woes.

Ophelia: May I cut my veins?

Hamlet: You see, I hate her, she brings out the worst of me! Destruction. Why do you want to cut your veins?

Ophelia: You don't love me!

Hamlet: Congratulations. What a blessing to you. That I don't love you. I won't destroy you. Good for you, Ophelia, take it from this—my heart—to these—your hands—good for you and for me—that we will not be able to hurt each other. Get thee to a nunnery. It has made me mad. Where is your father?

Ophelia: At home, my lord.

Hamlet:

Oh, yes, tell him to pledge allegiance to the American flag. I am Puerto Rican. You know what I mean. A radical who has no bait of truth—two flags—and no roots. I have not a single root left. They were eaten by a certain convocation of political worms. I mean, American and Puerto Rican. I mean, you and I have a common interest in the stock market. I mean, you know what I mean. We will have no more marriages. I am a stockbroker. Get a life! Get a job! Stop depending on my statehood. Make your own plans—impertinence to mine. Your needy arms are nothing but a sea of trouble surrounding my island. Keep your star! Keep your stripes! Get an independentista life! I said we will have no more marriages. It has made me mad. You say that you don't understand me—that I am mad. It's not that you don't understand me—it's that you know I caught you red-handed—not stealing fire from the Gods—but stooping as low as a sponger, a monger, a weasel, a picker, a stealer. It's not that you don't understand me. It's that I understand you all too well. You thought you could do your dirty deed unnoticed. But I noticed. I called you—murderer! And you—adulterer! You—accomplice to the crime! And you—you are a fishmonger! And you—you a spy! And for that reason, sir, I don't understand you? Nobody understands Hamlet? Liars, you all understand me! You all know what I am saying. You just pretend you don't because I am too real, too crude, too honest. I won't consent. I say no to you. I caught you. I know who you are. Don't think I don't know what you are doing.

Zarathustra: Don't convolute life more than it is already polluted. Take the dust out. I am coughing. I can hardly talk. The dust in my face. There must be a scholar around, revolting dust out of ideas and thoughts. They bring the worst out of me. Baggage and dust. I can't stop coughing. My tonsils.

Giannina: The cough will go as soon as the scholar leaves—whenever he appears he opens his pockets—and out of the pockets of his petticoat comes a rain of dust. Everybody coughs at once to chase the scholar out. Only one little phrase embroidered into the lining of his petticoat means something:

—*To thy own self be true.*

And it wasn't even said by him. But by another scholar who coughed the phrase full of dust until it broke apart upside down—now it means nothing—it says nothing—and it brings the phlegm out of your chest—and makes your throat sore.

Zarathustra: Why are we in *Hamlet?* Please tell me why we have to revisit the past.

Giannina:

Actors impose themselves. They want to make an event out of their wantonness. They impose their show business—as if they had any glory to show—just their small talent for showing off. I don't want to criticize, but since you asked me...

Zarathustra:

Why am I here? It's starting to feel as if we're in one of Wagner's operas. Wagner vs. Nietzsche. Homer vs. Plato. The philosopher is more important than the artist. In philosophy every line should have a reason to be. These actors are like scholars—coughers and spitters—spitting bubbles all over the stage—to show their enthusiasm in their enunciation and articulation—in spite of not meaning the words they spit. They don't know if the words they are spitting have any value—and the value they give to those words is the value they have heard a scholar cough. Scholars cough the value of the words because they don't know their worth.

Hamlet:

Do you think I always want to be Hamlet with Ophelia at my side—stealing the sun from my eyes? She wants to make me half an orange— half a banana. How would you feel if you are complete and all of a sudden someone comes in the name of love and says: you are no longer Hamlet but Hamlet and Ophelia. Only someone who is not complete would want to make a complete person incomplete—and when the person becomes incomplete with the other incomplete person at his side—then she says: now you are complete. But I was myself before she made me half. And I miss my other parts that she stole from me to complete her incompleteness. Give me back my Hamlet—my being. I was made of glass—and the crowds thought I was crazy—so they whispered under their breath—*he is mad*. But they left me alone—they knew I was fragile—so they didn't get close. I appreciated that they stood their distance—because I was made of glass. But she came too close—she saw I was made of glass—and asked: *can I sleep over?* I let her sleep over. She climbed under my sheets and took my pillow and put it under her head—and started hearing the rhythm of my breath and wrapped her limbs around me and said: *can I sneak even closer— can I capture that breath—can I make it beat faster?* And then she started intercepting my thoughts—as if they were phone calls—and my thoughts were intercepted by her phone calls— and soon I started worrying that I was made of ice and that I was melting—but I was made of glass and was breaking into many pieces. Before I had a unity. Now I am broken and I am not made of glass—I am naked and bleeding, and I am not one, but little pieces of the one I was— too many little pieces have gotten under my skin—she is one of them—she started sneaking under my sheets—now she is under my skin.

Giannina: Well, you know what Socrates says after Aristophanes speaks in *The Symposium*.

Hamlet: Who cares! I am hurting. Get her out!

Giannina: Ophelia?

Hamlet: I can't stand her. Get her out!

Giannina: He was referring to Aristophanes' theory that we were cut in half—we are not complete—we are half and half—and that is why we are always looking for our other half. But Socrates says no matter how incomplete we are—if a part of you is hurting—say—a tooth—ouch!—hurts you very much—you have to yank it out.

Hamlet: Yank her out!

Ophelia: You are mine, mine as the sea and wind when both contend which is the mightier.

Hamlet: The damage control is out of control. How can I recover what I was before you broke me in half? You gave me a prosthetic other half—one that is defective. You make me fragile—handle with care. Your weakness spreads like a computer virus. How can I get rid of your weakness—only if I make you strong—and I would make you strong if I could—but your weakness is stronger than my strength—and it's so debilitating that even though I am slim—in shape—not fat—your fatness—your blandness has infiltrated my shape, my slenderness—and transformed me into a bawd, a canopy, a fat prince—taking away my pride of being the glass of fashion and the mould of form. Your weakness will carry me and my kingdom away in your earthquake of a tsunami sweeping away all my villages and destroying my populace.

Segismundo: And they want to give me the weakling as wife? I will not marry Ophelia nor Giannina. Someone unheard of. Someone unknown. Someone I will recognize when I walk the streets of the world. Free from freedom. Free. I belong to all and to none. Why marry? No, I won't fall into that trap either. After being in a dungeon for more than a hundred years, you learn something: how to ventilate your brain. Everything in me will be free from freedom free.

Giannina: Do you understand what it means to feel unhappy?

Zarathustra: Everything is a river that leads to the sea. Don't stop the flow of things. Climb the mountains—walking ventilates your brain. Rain will fall—sometimes it will feel as if nothing is raining on your parade.

Giannina: But how do I distinguish? I am color blind.

Zarathustra: You must be missing a lot if you are color blind.

Giannina: I am missing my life. It's running ahead of me, frenetically. Where it is going, I don't know. But I am trying to get a grip on its wrist—to check its pulse. It has gone ahead. And that makes me happy. To run after it.

♫ *And when the night is cloudy*
There is still a light that shines on me
Shine until tomorrow
Let it be.

Zarathustra: This is what I tell you, Giannina, let it be, let the baby be. I will be the midwife.

Giannina: The baby will come out of her sandal.

Zarathustra: But you published it everywhere that he would come out of her vagina.

Giannina: He will tickle her foot with a feather. She will take off her sandal, shake the shackles on her left foot, and out of her sandal will come Segismundo. She won't even notice that he slipped out. She'll think that he is still under her skirt—but he won't be in the hem of her skirt—but between her toes.

Zarathustra: *Shhhhh!* Do you know how to keep a secret?

Giannina: No, I don't. Secrets are slippery. And he will slip away when she scratches her foot. Do you like it?

Zarathustra: I do like the absurd.

Giannina: Everybody thinks I will end with a bang—but I won't end with a whimper either—I will end with a greeting. Coming from another angle—one that is unexpected—and full of life—one that has carols and carrots—one that serenades—you expect it coming from the right, but it appears at the left foot as a puppy—drinking from the bowl of milk where Laches and Charmides licked and licked the milk from their whiskers like Felix the Cat—like the Phoenix—preparing a resurrection—like Lazarus coming back to tell you all—like myself arriving at the moment of bread and gratitude—when people are mellow with carols and carrots—when everybody is jumping like a rabbit that laughs like a goat—in Gotland—away from the United States of Banana—I will present my happiness as a tickle, as a feather that tickles the left foot, at the left side, I will come with a left memory—a memory that has not been left behind, but that tickles my left ear at dawn with a gratitude that has sheltered its eggs in a bowl full of milk and hope. Do not tell anybody my plans.

Zarathustra: These are not plans but confirmations.

Giannina: Segismundo will slip away with Hamlet, you, and me. The crown will be floating on the water—after the statue has hurled her crown into the river. All the people who were at the gala on the balconies of the crown will drown or swim away to the Jersey shore except you—the poet philosopher, me—the poet child,

Hamlet—the poet actor, and Segismundo—the poet statesman who will sail—on the four peaks of the crown—north, south, east, west—Zarathustra, Giannina, Hamlet, and Segismundo— the poet statesman who will be crowned Prince of the Isle of the Blessed, directing its energies and sailing against the wind and the sea toward the Isle of the Blessed where Segismundo was born to liberate his people from confinement and isolation, from embargos and diffuminations, from the bread and butter of daily routines—from isolation and confinement—from myself—I liberate myself from the United States of Banana.

Declaration of Independence

[Sailing to the Isle of the Blessed in the Statue's crown.]

Hamlet: Watch out, she is coming after us.

Giannina: Who? Your mother?

Hamlet: No, she is drowning in the waters of lilies with Ophelia. Basilio and Oliver are swimming toward the city that never sleeps, leaving my mother and Ophelia drowning in the waters of lilies.

Giannina: Look at their hypocrisy. The way they bashed Teddy Kennedy. I always thought that we should throw all the presidential candidates into the Chappaquiddick. With their wives—in cars—drowning. To see which of them would save his wife in order to become the president. Bravo, Lady Liberty, for throwing the crown into the river. And the torch, give it to another country or to another human being who will create a fire, a bonfire.

Statue: I'll give it to you. Let me run for my life. I have to safe my ass. Before the authorities arrest me and reconstruct me. I don't want to be reconstructed after this deconstruction. I feel like a crane on a demolition site.

Giannina: Go save them!

Hamlet: No, did I ask them to follow me?

Giannina: We can't let them die!

Hamlet: No, they were already dead when we met them again. I was referring to the spirit of Liberty—look how our crown is sailing toward the Isle of the Blessed—nobody is steering—it's the wind of liberty driving us—without grudges on its back—without camels—as a newborn baby—no obstacles—we have no more obstacles—now that we have liberated the poet statesman from the dungeon of liberty.

Zarathustra: I will stay for a while on the Isle of the Blessed.

Giannina: Segismundo, let me give you as your new bastion the Quixotesque ideals: love, poetry, arms, liberty, and justice. Rule with these ideals.

Segismundo: Arms? What do I need arms for?

Giannina: You think the U. S. of Banana won't fight tooth and nail to get Puerto Rico back?

Segismundo: They never wanted us.

Giannina: You never know what you want until you lose it.

Segismundo: But you made a deal with China when I declared the independence of Puerto Rico. I upgraded your rank from performer, eternal performer in the United States of Banana, to ambassador of the Republic of Puerto Rico. You were schmoozing with the photographer Cato Lein who said:

> —*I come as a messenger of the crown to take pictures of the immortals:*
>
> Giannina (put the donkey first so it won't get spooked)
> Hamlet
> Zarathustra
> Segismundo

Cato Lein: Here on the balcony of the torch *(click, click)*. And here beside the golden flame *(click, click)*.

Giannina: Please, take a photo of Rubén Darío and me.

Cato Lein: *Click, click.*

Giannina: And of me and Antonin Artaud, please.

Cato Lein: *Click, click.*

Giannina: Wait a minute, there is Darío talking to Vallejo and Neruda. I need a photo of us four for the annals of your collection of the Immortals. Darío, Giannina, Neruda, Vallejo.

Cato Lein: *Click, click*

Giannina: César, you are *el fantoche del dolor*—a jack-in-the-box, the movement of your spirit—that is what I took from you. The more they push us down—and this society—look at all of them—grazing like brown cows—the brownies—all of us—*mestizos*—all of us—the rich and the poor—grazing grass—like cows—while the prodigal son tries to pass the elephant through the eye of the needle. How hard for the rich to pass the needle through the eye of the elephant—and how easy for them to push us down:

                —Today I like life much less.

But jack-in-the-box comes up again, surprising all the fools in the crown:

                —But I always love life!

My poet is a jack-in-the-box—it always rises—after it has been kept down—and put down—it always rises like the Ave Phoenix to announce the resurrected glory—of the independence of Puerto Rico from the U. S. of Banana. It is my own liberation from the mentality of making money for a living—instead of living—and of the utility of everything that has no utility in a practical world. I am interested in the mechanics of the spirit. I have a jingle bell that wants to get out of the metal bars that are imprisoning my jingle. But my jingle sounds best when it hits the obstacle that doesn't let my jingle jangle. And the mermaids sing—and the sailors plug their ears not to hear—and some people cough in protest.

Neruda: Congratulations! You are already an ambassador like me, a diplomat. Giannina, talk to the ambassadors of China. They are there in the corner nodding at us. They want something from us—and we want something from them.

Giannina: Who are they?

Neruda: Hu and How. Come, I'll introduce you. And this, Hu and How, is the ambassador of the Republic of Puerto Rico to the United Nations.

Giannina: Hu and How—from the Republic of China to the Republic of Puerto Rico—from a bowl of rice to a bowl of beans—from a *litchi* to a *quenepa*. I love *chinas mandarinas*—I eat them all the time. On behalf of the Republic of Puerto Rico I wish to visit Beijing to strike a deal now that we are celebrating the independence of Puerto Rico.

Hu: This could be World War III.

Giannina: Isn't it true that what the Chinese want is power,
                        not money—that you use money to get power—
                        but money is just a vehicle?

How: Who told you that?

Giannina: I have been in conversation with Hu's delega-
                        tion about how to strike a deal and come across
                        as a messenger of peace. Hu said—China wants
                        power—Puerto Rico wants liberty—the United
                        States of Banana wants money. I propose that
                        China strike a deal with the United States of
                        Banana—saying: Yankee dollar—we pardon your
                        debt to China. Pardon only half of it—make them
                        depend on you still—Wishy-Washy. Puerto Rico's
                        liberty costs less than you think. So hold them
                        accountable still—*(wink wink)*—a chain to the
                        sandals of Lady Liberty so that she won't come
                        running after us with bills of accountability and
                        debts and constraints. You think, Hu and How,
                        that they won't accept the deal—the payment of
                        half of the U.S. debt to China in exchange for the
                        liberty of Puerto Rico? I assure you that you won't
                        hear another peep about the Dalai Lama—nor
                        about any human rights violations—if you par-
                        don half—not an inch nor a quarter more. You
                        will get the power you want. You will be revered
                        by all Latin America and Europe and Africa
                        for avoiding World War III and validating the

Declaration of Independence of the Republic of Puerto Rico by confirming as a statement of fact—be concrete—by striking a trilateral agreement between China and the U. S. of Banana and the Republic of Puerto Rico—each gets what they want—each gets power, pesos, and liberty.

[Ringing of bells]

> ♫ *Tiling, tiling, tilong*
> *Oye que bonito este cantar*
> *De mis campanitas de cristal*
> ♫ *Tiling, tiling, tilong*
> *Solo para ti*
> *Solo para mí*
> *Campanitas de cristal*

[Puerto Rican National Hymn]

> ♫ *La tierra de Borinquen,*
> *Donde he nacido yo,*
> *Es un jardín florido,*
> *De mágico primor*

And for more than a hundred years they wanted to turn us from gold into copper—from china into plastic—and they wanted us to be a sad colony—oppressed by a minority who ignored that the majority was oppressed by *pan, tierra y libertad*—and without liberty—and without bread—and without land—they turned us—the rich port of Puerto Rico—into the poor port of Puerto Pobre—because without liberty there is no wealth (this is the contradiction of the worm). Now we can start our negotiations with the whole wide world. Not only for the United States of Banana, and in the United States of Banana, and with the United States of Banana. The embargo has harmed our sovereignty. It has silenced our way of thinking. The world has not heard us dealing with the issues of the world, nor reacting to the news of the world: the good, the bad, and the ugly. We have let the United States of Banana speak for us—even though they were speaking against us. We were fighting for them in wars against people that we had more in common with than with the United States of Banana. We forgot who we were and what we wanted. We forgot how to make our own choices—in our own interests. We looked at them with shock and awe. We didn't understand their language. We thought they could lead us to freedom, but they led us into feardom, not freedom. We thought we had a good deal—but the deal was good for them—not for us. We thought—we can't make it by ourselves—we are too little—too petite. Cuba will eat us up. Russia will eat us up. China will eat us up. We are better off under the tax shelter of their umbrella—under the tortoise shell—let's forget we exist—let's make them better than what they are—let's sing and dance for them—let's give them our services—our armies—our police—our babies—and our doormen—to open the doors for them. And little by little they threw us out of the cities, closing the doors on us. We were dancing and singing, trying to make them happy—it was hard—because they don't understand love—they understand violence, rage, intemperance—and inflexibility. Wanting always to be the boss—they were negotiating with other countries and blockading us. We were angry. We planted a bomb in the Oval Office—destroyed national treasures—took a shit on the White House lawn. What we wanted was to put our own interests first—to deal with the world directly—not with you in front and us behind. You were obsessed with external affairs. And we were never part of your internal affairs. And our votes when we voted never counted for nothing. Counting for nothing—let me tell you—degraded our standards of expectations. We expected very little of ourselves—so little that we forgot we had a self. Who has a self here—we don't—we don't know who we are. And then you gave us three choices: Wishy, Wishy-Washy, and Washy. But we never chose to be mashed, fried, or baked by you. Three ways, three languages. The traffic passing by *la guagua aérea* and the exchanges of money, violence, and words kept us from seeing that we could cross over to the other side—that we didn't have to keep eating our entrails in the middle. And you praised those who thought we were less and not more—those who thought we were minorities—those who made us little— and the ones who belittled us—those were the ones whom you gave your ear to—the ones who knew the art of making little what is big and big what is little—the ones who alienated us more— the ones who thought little of themselves—and you thought you could continue belittling us until you transformed our flesh into dust—a dust that can make you cough—but a cough is a little protest—against a strong wind.

The powers of the world are shifting. Look at the crown moving toward the Isle of the Blessed— the wind is moving the crown—effortlessly— willingly—with laughter—sneezes and hiccups—with good will—this is what you have forgotten, the good will—what wills with salt and sand—what tender loving wills—what doesn't reduce—what doesn't confine—what sails— what smells good and healthy and wealthy and wise. You tried to make us poor—and you fabricated consent all around the world—through the bad breath of your gossip—that we are poor—and you neglected to say that we have more—not less—that we are multiplying our wine and cheese and our bread—that we have so many healthy and wealthy puppies—and they are crying and speaking in tongues—and you act as if we didn't exist, ignoring the fact

that our growth made you less—and not more.
And you dictate from the podium of the United
Nations of Banana new world orders, but we're
going to make no use of those world orders that
were formulated on false classifications. And
you kept telling us:

> —*You are on the borderline—we almost*
> *failed you—but we let you pass this time.*

And when you let us pass this time—as if you
were doing us a favor—we slipped into the
crown and we started navigating—away from
you—toward the Isle of the Blessed. No regrets,
no sour feelings—no hard feelings—without
grudges and bad energy—just with love—we
say again: thank you for your good services rendered to the Banana Republic of Puerto Rico.
From now on, we will deal with our own issues
in our own way. We don't need your services
any longer. You are fired from Puerto Rico. We
can manage better by ourselves—and if we need
good services—there are plenty of countries in
the world—including you—who will be more
than happy to strike a deal.

Hu: Don't let anyone convince you that you are
               poor.

Giannina: I am not poor. I am very, very rich. Puerto Rico
               is a rich port. Fruit falls off our trees. We have

fishes in the sea. The Russians are coming to teach us how to produce caviar. Puerto Rican caviar like Puerto Rican rum.

How:

You are letting the Russians ashore?

Giannina:

♫ *Cuando a sus playas llegó Colón.*
Exclamó lleno de admiración:
Oh! Oh! Oh!
Esta es la linda tierra que busco yo.

We belong to none and to all. And believe me, we'll try anything. Before the U. S. of B. mass-produced any merchandise—they always tested it first in Puerto Rico. If Puerto Rico buys it—roller blades, cell phones, digital cameras—so will the rest of the world. We are vanguardistas. That is why the best psychics of the world are Puerto Rican. We don't want enemies—we want friends.

Zarathustra:

Don't try too hard to accommodate. They'll squeeze your consideration.

Giannina:

I am not an orange juice. Although I know how to distinguish fresh-squeezed from Tropicana. Miami is Tropicana, defrosted from a can. San Juan is fresh-squeezed from the fruit of a tree.

Hu:

Could we squeeze you?

Giannina: No, you can't. Just pay the debt. And trade with us. You give us a bowl of rice. We give you a bowl of beans. You give us *litchi*. We give you *quenepa*. What I like of your people is that when you work with my people—you learn to speak our language. And you learn fast. With the U. S. of B. there was no such relationship. Don't you think that after a century of American colonization—Puerto Ricans should be fluent in English? They wanted us to be stray dogs—not belonging—not forming part—not incorporating—not given a chance—and when they gave us a chance—it was against all odds. I went to first grade in an American school. And I told my grandmother: get me out of there. It's alien to what I do in my house. I speak Spanish—why should I be taught in a language alien to myself. This I understood when I was six years old.

How: So why are you writing in English?

Giannina: I write the way I live. I could not write all my life in Spanish living in New York. I am a medium of thoughts. Segismundo, this is Hu, prime minister of China. She is the only Chinese person I know, so I had to name her prime minister. But this is the way things start. By naming them. And this, Hu, is Segismundo. You're dying to do business with him.

Hu: Segismundo, let us form new power structures.

Segismundo: Not world orders. Please don't divide and
                 conquer. You divide so much and conquer so
                 little—and your divisions make it impossible
                 to remember that we had something to say
                 direct and to the heart of things. We thought
                 we could do without a nation because we had
                 big brother protecting us from hostile and for-
                 eign nations, but big brother never protected
                 us—it neglected us—it said: we don't care for
                 your welfare, so we'll put you on welfare—and
                 they despised us for what they were doing to
                 us—because they didn't want to deal with our
                 little problem—a problem of the kitchen—not
                 a problem of external affairs. Every problem
                 has to be dealt with—especially the little prob-
                 lems—the ones we dismiss as unessential—as
                 not affecting our welfare—but I am affecting
                 your welfare because I'm on welfare, and I don't
                 want to be on welfare. I have no context—I am
                 not a priority—I am a minority—that is what
                 they say—and I say—my priorities were laid
                 back as minorities because they had no jobs and
                 they learned to be laid back and delayed, and
                 they developed a second constitution different
                 to the first constitution and both constitutions
                 developed even with an arrested libido—an
                 arrested constitution.

[On the high seas.]

Zarathustra:	Let it be. Let it float in the water.
Giannina:	We're getting there, aren't we?
Zarathustra:	Yes, we are. Where is independence?
Giannina:	I don't need it anymore. That's how it always is. Once you get it—independence—it stops being a constitution, an obsession—it becomes an accomplishment—a feather in your cap.
Zarathustra:	So, you're not a nationalist anymore?
Segismundo:	I was never a nationalist. I wanted freedom.
Giannina:	What will be our next stop?
Segismundo:	The one that never stops sailing.
Giannina:	I think we're going too far. We might have missed our destination. Weren't we supposed to land by now?
Segismundo:	We are supposed to liberate the islanders from not knowing who they are.
Giannina:	Save me from not knowing who I am?

Segismundo: It's morning. They are waiting for us—the whole island has opened its arms to embrace us. We gave them higher expectations—now they are expecting us with arms open—to have a secretary of state—a voice in the United Nations—embassies all over the world to welcome people like us. They are starting to feel again—as a people—as a flag—as a nation—with a monetary system that belongs to them. They feel that everything will settle when the ship gets there with arms to pick a fight.

Giannina: This is an embarkation, not a destination. Destinies are set forever, and we are set to sail and depart—to navigate—to say goodbye.

Zarathustra: Let it be, let the baby be, and float toward the Isle of the Blessed. All those in the crown are drowning—and wondering why they are drowning.

Giannina: They were drowning in their debts—so many creditors—up to the neck—and then they got hold of lawsuits and investment banks—and they called it: development. But nobody developed out of development—except debts that floated over the waters on plastic credit cards. All of the ones who made it to the shores were wet to start with—though they claimed they had never experienced anything like it. But here what is considered experience is another

226

plot—to add to the narration of events that don't count—a lot of waves—and so little that counted. And the stories were broken into so many little scratches and snatches—when I started counting the scratches—I stopped counting how many pages. What do you do for a living? As if I had to do something to recover from not living a life that I should have lived (but there is no but).

Zarathustra: Where poets have achieved the most distinction is in the realm of lust and indolence. They have not discovered the tones.

Giannina: Well, I'm here—talking to you—because I have discovered the tones. I speak in tongues.

Zarathustra: So much imperfection made event.

Giannina: Are you referring to poets who turn sneezes, hiccups, farts, and belches into poems? Because we stay in the realm of the senses. We perceive and we are deceived—Descartes would say. Our cogito is as vibrant as the colors of the peacock when he spreads his tail.

Zarathustra: You are trying to enchant. Imperfections are full of charm.

Giannina: What's wrong with charm? Charm is the strength of the daemon—the halo of affirmation—the installation of light. Even without your instruments of knowledge—your sharp edges—I can develop my charm without perfect clarity. I can be a clairvoyant and shine through. Clarity is impurity shining through the imperfections. The spider web, the ants, the cockroaches, the flies. Do I have to kill them all in order to make an event—or can the event happen with all the imperfections coming through? Why would I want Oliver Exterminator to kill cockroaches when I myself am considered a cockroach?

Zarathustra: You are complacent with your imperfections, indulging yourself in the indolence of moles, calling them beauty marks to beautify the imperfections—which is what poets do—because they love what is imperfect and feel satisfied talking about shadows on the wall—without looking back at the light that shines through the hole of the cave—because the poet is always a big fat sex—where he sits—on a rock—rocking his feelings out of a little thought—trying to find a new geometry in those patterns that deceive the sight. The patterns are shadow puppets that disappear when the sun sets—because they never existed—they lived in the realm of the becoming—not in the realm of the being.

Giannina: What is a being that never becomes?

Zarathustra: A becoming.

Giannina:

Like a big fat orgasm—the organism that becomes a being—when it moves out of its own will—toward a unity—a duende. That depends on the energy of the charm—if it gets to the head—where the daemon lives—and doesn't stay in the throat—where the duende sings a song of charm. There in the throat—or there in the head—the charm of the daemon has a prophecy to decipher. As far as I know—and I don't know much—I know a little bit—about a lot of things—but not enough about you—so what can I do—what can I do with what I know—I know it's not enough—enough for a master of ceremonies like you. My master of ceremonies, my anagnorisis, myself.

Philosophers, poets, lovers. The powers of the world are shifting. Culture is becoming more relevant than politics. Cities more relevant than nations. Continents more relevant than nations. But continents less relevant than cities. Languages more relevant than nations. Languages are alive. Nations are dead. I should not be concerned about what is alive or dead. Yes, I should. I want what is alive—not what is dead—following what is dead delays my path. Creation is taking over representation—by representation I mean also narration, plot, descriptions—and all the paraphernalia of information for analphabetism that adds more garbage (less meaning). Creation means discovery of a new reality that exists but that has not yet been noticed. The word is alive again. The speaking word. The verbs are in revolt—a revolt of the masses against the representation that has always been the main weapon of the state. The power is not in the state but in the culture of the people, by the people, and for the people. The media works for the state and against the culture of the people, by the people, and for the people. Culture is always about food and language—about what makes people hungry and alive—what makes them vibrant—the colors of the rainbow—the peacocks, the buffalos, and the cows. This culture that is arriving to New York through New (Ark) airport is a culture of philosophers, poets, and lovers. Love is what is new—so old and necessary—the old god that interchanges values, meaning, sentimentality, food, and languages—the missing link in this culture of destruction and death. The culture of newspapers, of information, of journalism—of Starbucks, Kinko's, Barnes & Noble—this culture of the present as here and now—is dying—is already dead—is the dead horse that died in the middle of the stage—don't kick a dead horse—and why not—why did it dare to die in the middle of the stage—attention-getter—and then it refuses to leave the stage—in the middle. Let's bring a crane to take it away.

Giannina Braschi

The stage (the state) has been for centuries representing itself—governments, kings, queens—prime ministers and mass murderers—poisoners and characters that are thorough—that follow through—that have the ability to become themselves—and that are logic—and that can be analyzed through the logic of demolition and death—through the representation of the state on the stage. Kings and queens of the world, prime ministers and secretaries of the stage—when you represent us—putting a cage of teeth in front—with your damned smile—we look behind the bars of your teeth—and beyond your stage—through those holes—the graces are flying—they are telling us—hear the cicadas—they are singing freely—and they are incapable of representing—they are there to be caught—to be held in hand—to let us tell the story again—the story about a multitude that we lump-summed into one whole mass—packed in polls and statistics—but the cicadas and swans of prophecies are singing—and the jack-in-the-box is jumping out of the box—and the jingle-bell is bouncing against the wall—and the sound has nothing to do with what you give us as food for thoughts. This is not about representing you, but about creating ourselves—about finding ways to communicate with what is not isolated and confined to a product dated by the market of isolation and death. A product confined to a canned sardine future has no

231

bright future because it has no sun—and no way out. The powers of the world are shifting from death to creation. Our thoughts are dying. We have to ventilate our brains. What you tell us is—is not it anymore. And you thought—maybe you never thought—I am giving you too much credit when I said you thought—but maybe you did think we would always be those players that merely sit—sedated by Prozac—a hundred years of plots—to silence our voices—to tell us that we were what we are not—mama grandes and papa grandes—and grandpapas—and primas and prima donnas—to isolate us—in Macondo—and confine us to the stigma of being bananas—well, bananas for all—bring the bananas for the United States of Banana—and bring apples and oranges for the United Nations of Banana—and share a slice of our bread of isolation. And stop describing the fruit I see in front of my eyes in primary colors. Step aside—let me see the yellow with my own eyes—I don't need your glasses—I trust my sight. Describing life as if I had not put my finger on fire—and gotten burned. Experience, the mother of all the eggs that my chickens lay. And when you repeat this is good—and when you impose on us what you think is good—and we say to ourselves—we don't think so—that voice that says no, but says yes—the voice that affirms an inaugura-tion with scissors that cut ribbons—and with benediction and good will—and senses open to transformations. I want new thoughts—not more plots—plots don't think—they knead the dough of strategic plans—making the bread plain—uniform—more than plain—plain is good—but uniformity of thought brings no thinking. And why does your voice have to be over the narration—putting us to sleep with your analysis of analphabetism, and polls and statistics that plot to mass destruct our wishes come true, killers of emotions, of poets, of philosophers, of lovers.

Emotions are back. And emotions are talking. And we listen because we are open people— open to the world—open to the streets—open to the doors that are open. We enter *como Pedro por su casa*—we eat—we pass by—where you can't love—you better pass by—and that is what I have been doing—passing by—because it was impossible to love what I saw—and I have high expectations of love—when I love I really love— but I can't love what wants to destroy me—it's as simple as that—what leaves me in the margins—seated and sedated by drugs of equanimity—when something is happening that I know is happening—that the emotions of all these people who were seated are coming back to life—to haunt their lives—to live anew—the blessing of becoming what we are.

I cannot tell you what I feel because you are a character (say, a poet—an established poet) and why should I tell you how I feel so that you can use my feelings in your poetry. Who then would be the poet—the one who uses the feelings—or the one who feels them inside? Why would I who am feeling this atrocious sensation of disembodiment also want to play the role of a poet—it would disempowered my emotions—it would make them conscious—it would stop running—the river—with a different feeling in every lane of the drive and dive. This is what I understand as me—something that hasn't happened yet—but that will not happen in the character that represents the state of mind of a character called poet—because there is no state/stage in the poet—just an open mind—open to the traffic jam.

Not even the poet represents the me that I have inside—so you—character/poet who through the centuries has tried to represent the role that I supposedly have inside—you—poet—cannot understand the feelings that are swimming in the river of my mind—and not every current that runs passes the same lane of thoughts. It is this rebellious being that has come to the surface in all of us in the audience who have been misrepresented by those of you who don't understand the transformations that have happened in our *derrumbaciones*—in those states where

chance and expectation have been the measurement of the mathematics of affliction—and
the relation has been broken between creation
and representation, love and fiction—and the
reality of packing meat in the meatpacking dis-
trict. The characters—all the world's a stage—
and all those characters that appear on those
stages—merely players—are all dead—even the
poet as a character that represents me—there
is nobody representing me on that stage—
the stage is also out of character with itself—
it hasn't realized that the stage/the state/the
face that you are giving me—as the face of my
body—has no relation to my body—it doesn't
need to have any relation to the body—as long
as it represents the body efficiently (for the people, of the people, by the people). The body is
where the voices dwell—not on the stage/state,
but in the body where the stomach growls when
it hears the characters thoroughly representing
themselves (shamelessly)—who do they think
they are representing—we think—not I—and
we hear the jingle bell of our poetry touch the
wall—and there is no correlation—no objective correlative—no relation to the thought that
dwells inside the measurement of expectation
and chance. Exception is the rule—and there
is no ruler—but the exception to the rule that
kills the origin. Originality is to go back to the
origins—and that's why I go back to the exceptional—what is extra—what gives gifts—gener-

osity and light. The writing that goes overboard and over borders—and that is on the edge of breaking—and finds a light—and beams. The writing that is not good but extra—because it has extra points, extra credit—and it goes higher and lower with charm—and love is essential— it is the driving force—but good writing is not good—it's normal—and the norm is useless at this time. Professional writers who don't commit mistakes of judgment spell with the ruler of the rule, but have no knowledge of the thing— the is that is—the being that shines and beams like a bean—the struggle can count on enemies and friends—so do the conflicts and the grievances—but the exception to the rule—that sapphire in the mud—the useless writing that never wrote to find a job, that never found a job with the counting of the rule as a ruler—the beam that shines like a bean—the exceptional that never said: I earned it, look how hard I work. I would prefer, being an athlete of the heart, to exercise the body of work—constant toning and thinning of the body of work— through the scrutiny of the saying—the weighing of what counts—does it have meaning—is it a trip through the groves of knowledge—are we picking oranges with a bowl—licking the bowl until it is bald and bold—empty and full of the imperfections of the leftovers—that are left—to signal to a different bean and beam in the soup of lentils—the beans that are left—the lefties

of the leftovers are regrouping themselves—
and confabulating a progress—to create a new
situation—a good situation for me—one of the
leftovers—thanks for not eating me—for letting
me exist as a bean, a beam, a ray—a leftover—a
trace that stands alone in the bowl—with this
trace I create a stroke—my strokes are generous—I don't amplify them—no, thank you—I
don't need amplifiers—to amplify my strokes in
front of the TV cameras—or to rewind them—
to show the strokes of the athlete of the heart—
the heart has been marching to the rhythm of
its own beat—slowly—not cautiously—stroking the muscles of the heart—don't think the
brain is a leftover—I also stroke the brain—with
the same fingers that I use to play the piano—
ten at a time of decadence—but each stroke is
a beat that marches to its own rhythm—and it
beams—when it wants to beam—in the beginning—it strives—it strokes more boldly later
on—when it figures it has a shape and an organ
to play—and then it finds a dwelling inside that
heart called Valentino—the heart of the poet
actor—the heart of Antonin Artaud—my poet
actor, my athlete of the heart—the stroker—
the one who strokes my heart—the one who
wants love among the others who want knowledge and deference and magnitude—and the
powerful one is stroking the strike—strike
one—and those who understand are not the
ones who get to the knowledge—the ones who

understand are hearing the beats of the heart—
they are beaming like a bean inside a bowl of
rice—and I beam my smile that is missing its
two front teeth—shamelessly—shame never
was made when the stroker strokes the home
run—run—the athlete of the heart—Valentino—the heart of hearts—was waving—run—
Gia—run—and I had to run backwards before
I jumped forward—and my strokes were generous and magnanimous—to leap into the air—
and stay there—jumping in the air—without a
platform—and not feeling the weight nor the
altitude of the air—weightless—and without
air—jumping in that gap—that provokes other
strokes to strike a bean with a racket—and no
ball—everything is in the air—and it should
stay in the air—without the final resolution of
a punch or a struggle or a conflict—in the air.

Declaration of War

[Disembarking at the Port of Old San Juan. News ticker reads: Yanks Invade San Juan.]

Giannina: Waging war against Puerto Rico now instead of picking a fight with someone their own size! Did they invade Russia or China? No, they invade Puerto Rico! I told you, Segismundo, that you needed arms, didn't I?

Segismundo: They'll vilify me, and I owe it all to you. You fired them. You went too far. You didn't have to fire them.

Giannina: It's the only language they understand—the language of office control freak. I read their dirty minds and fired them before they could fire us. But now they are pointing their guns at us—neither El Morro nor La Fortaleza will be able to defend us against their weapons of mass destruction. We have been through a lot lately. First, the invasion by Cuba—that was a big trauma for the Puerto Rican people—and now this invasion by the United States of Banana— this is too much, this is too, too much.

Zarathustra: Every country has the right to defend itself.

Giannina: But we don't even have weapons. Our weapons are feathers, and pens, and tongues—and eggs.

Zarathustra: They'll vilify you like they vilified me—for creating fire where there was only water to quench the fire.

Giannina: I had to stoke the fire of the Cuban Revolution, the Chinese Revolution, the Russian Revolution, the French Revolution. *Le Monde* is saying who would have thought that such a tiny island would kick the United States in the ass—the ass that not even Russia or China or Germany dared to kick. David vs. Goliath. And David beat Goliath.

Zarathustra: And now all Latin America is preparing their *armada invencible* to defend *la isla bonita*. Chávez is the leader with Kirchner close behind—and Ortega and Morales side by side—in defense of *la isla bonita*. Puerto Rico had all the right to declare its independence.

Segismundo: But not all the *boricuas* agreed with her. More diplomacy, please!

Giannina: If you know they are going to shoot you, you fire first in self-defense. I fired the shot at their

Achilles' heel and sent them to the unemploy-ment line.

Zarathustra: It was a slap in the face from someone they con-sider minor.

Giannina: They say it is illegal.

Zarathustra: What is illegal?

Giannina: The declaration—and the firing. They are com-ing after us with their weapons of mass destruc-tion.

Zarathustra: They should wage war against their equals.

Giannina: They never wage wars against their equals. They are afraid of China—but not of Puerto Rico. Climb this coconut tree. Throw this coconut at G.I. Joe. American soldiers are always cam-ouflaged as reptiles belly-crawling through the desert dunes. Well, the desert dunes are now the sands of el Caribe Hilton. And they are look-ing for us—poets, philosophers, and lovers. I always knew the war on terror would turn out to be war on poets, war on philosophers, war on lovers. Throw another coconut at G.I. Joe's head. What are we going to do with these reptiles as enemies? They let Castro and Chávez pass—but not us—no, not us. Why? Why are they after us? And not after them—I thought—if they can get away with it, of course, I can get away. But look where we are—on top of a coconut tree—the symbol of statehood. The extermination of Oliver Exterminator—didn't I prophesize that they would come after us like cockroaches? Reptiles against cockroaches. Throw another coconut.

Segismundo: I don't know how. I always said: I don't know how.

Giannina: Call our allies to defend us. The leaders of the first, second, and third worlds. Take my cell phone.

Segismundo: I don't have their numbers.

Giannina: We have to create some order here. We have to create a school of followers the way Protagoras and Socrates did. But not Homer—they say even his lover ignored him—because it was boring to live with a storyteller who narrated the mirror. But Protagoras and Socrates had followers—and created schools of thoughts—and people really loved them. We need a crowd of followers—it's the best way to establish alliances.

Segismundo: What we need are bodyguards!

Giannina: No, followers, a school of graceful followers—and grateful also—so they thank us. Ingratitude, oh, another coco.

Zarathustra: *Qué brutos.* They didn't even realize we were behind the coconuts—and they left thinking that coconut trees are dangerous. An eagle dropped a turtle on Aeschylus's head and killed him—but when a coconut cracked open a reptile's skull, it didn't kill the reptile—it just broke open the coco—and out came the juice—so the reptiles drank the juice—ate the coco—and left to do their mission impossible. To hunt down the philosophers and poets who were sunbathing at different resorts. Protagoras was at el Conquistador. Parmenides at el Caribe Hilton. Zeno at el Hotel Condado. Socrates at el Hotel San Juan. And I was at el Convento.

Giannina: I hid behind the coconuts laying poetic eggs. The strategy was to lure the reptiles into the resorts so they would destroy their own constructions. How lazy can they be? They come here to vacate their businesslike mentalities in their temples of laziness—and then they accuse the natives of being lazy when the lazy ones are the tourists—lying belly-up on sun beds—showing their navels and nipples—the men and the women—hanging around like they do at work—hanging around—acting as if they were doing something—as if getting a tan were doing something. The rays of the sun, it's true, saps their energy—they feel sleepy—so they go back to their rooms—and spend more time sleeping in mushy cushions—too drained from the sun to make love—and when night falls, they go to casinos to play with play money—and act as if they had real money—and during the day they drink rum and Coca-Cola in their bathing suits—with all their white chest hair hanging there like sweaty polar bears—drinking piña coladas and eating hamburgers and French fries with ketchup. They feel rich for being able to spend a few days in a resort being lazy. Just look at their unexercised bellies—the bellies are jumping boards—I could jump on those bellies like I jump on beds—for the sheer joy of it. And then they say Puerto Ricans are lazy—because they project onto the Puerto Rican people the laziness that they display when they come to the island. But the ones who are lazy are the reptiles belly-crawling through the sand dunes of el Caribe Hilton—

drinking rum and Coca-Cola
working for the Yankee dollar.

And they keep asking—these Yankee dollars—what's going on?—when they call you on their cell phones—chewing gum—they spread their virus of laziness through their lazy gizmos that are lazier than their big bulky bellies that rise like a Russian mountain—and fall in love—you really need to be crazy to fall in love instead of rise in love—if you fall it's because you are not rising—you are falling into an American state of mind—like a balloon when it's losing all its air—but they don't lose their air—they snore instead of screaming—because screaming takes too much air out of their lungs and the rage mounts the mountain and they say to themselves—calm down—

drinking rum and Coca-Cola
working for the Yankee dollar.

And then they fly back to Cincinnati and bad-mouth Puerto Rico. What do they say: Puerto Ricans are lazy. But they exercised all their laziness—never leaving the resort—afraid of being mauled by a Puerto Rican dog—or afraid of being assaulted by a Puerto Rican thug—or simply because they are lazy, accept it, Americans are the laziest people in the whole wide world—

drinking rum and Coca-Cola
working for the Yankee dollar.

And after their vacation at the resort that erases stress—or so they say—they need to erase from the blackboard the fights they could not have with their wives because they snored their screams when they got drunk—it was too hard to handle the dragon lady—fierce—and so he tells her: calm down! You party animal, you social butterfly! Go shopping! While he enters the beach with a yellow towel covering his testicles—she enters the mall—both smiling, but their unhappiness is so big that it could take a whole day of sunscreen and earphones not to hear the other say what they don't want to hear—

> *drinking rum and Coca-Cola*
> *working for the Yankee dollar.*

At first it sounds like magic—drinking rum and Coca-Cola—burning their cheeks and flashing their baby teeth—as a testifier of happiness. Calm down! Everything is alright, baby. And the earphones are louder—and the louder the merrier—drinking cappuccino from Starbucks—where tall means small—because digressions are recessions—and know that if you walk backwards—like a crab—it brings bad luck—to go back to where you started—

> *drinking rum and Coca-Cola*
> *working for your own nasty dollar.*

And then all of a sudden, a real nasty person comes out from the yellow towel around his waist—and reveals an unhappiness that instead of screaming has been snoring all night long— but in the morning while he takes the elevator to the lobby he says—good morning—and drinks a cappuccino from tall means small—and reads in the *Times* about a woman who jumped on a cardinal who fell on the pope and knocked him down—and a reporter threw a shoe at the president—and another threw a punch at the prime minister and broke his jaw and nose—and the power is shifting—like the tsunami of an insurrection by the people, for the people, of the people. Nasty people are getting nastier. The brew is brewing. The coming insurrection. And the natives are also there sunbathing in the same resort. I'm talking about the children of the colonizers who frequent the hotels—not as tourists but where society meets society—where locals take their wives and kids—because they prefer to be with tourists than with natives who are mulattos, because no, they are not mulattos, or so they think, they are the children of *conquistadores* and *exterminadores*. What a match when a conquistador marries an exterminator—they become owners of newspapers, shopping malls, mental asylums, restaurants, banks. I am one of those children, raised in el Caribe Hilton where I played tennis and ate hamburgers and french fries and fried chicken and fried calamari and drank Coca-Cola—and sunbathed on their private beaches—and danced in their nightclubs—and I saw the rupture and the excuse—and how upsetting it can be when the strong culture is controlled by domineering politics—it creates the sadness of a sad ballad—like the ballad of the sad café—in New Orleans—a sad city—

where the majority are oppressed by a minority—and the joie de vivre of French and black culture is oppressed by another culture—that is minor—it creates bad conscience, it takes the blessedness of the blessed, the being can't be completed—because it is repressed and subdued by the rum and Coca-Cola of working for the Yankee dollar.

Giannina Braschi

Hotel El Exterminador

In Fajardo they have just finished constructing the most luxurious hotel called Hotel El Exterminador. It was built by the husband of one of the daughters of the owner of Hotel El Conquistador. Hotel El Exterminador is famous for having as its most famous guest—Oliver Exterminator who exterminates with a spray of raid everything that is related to race and sex—and if it has no relation to sex and race—it's because it hasn't come out of the closet yet—because every figure, every equation, every mathematical confabulation can be eradicated by a spray of raid on sex and race—through the eye of the elephant the needle of a one-track mind—always with blinders—always a steel trap—a mousetrap—a mouthtrap—to catch with the extermination of race and sex the highly suspicious code red of high alert—calm down—you are on a movie set of gigolos—good-for-nothings—only if the cause is serving the cause of the raid formula of blank verse—fill in the blanks—polls and statistics—standards—and good-for-nothings sprayed by the raid of sex and race.

Glazed Donut

Hotel El Exterminador is called the Glazed Donut because it's round like a glazed donut with a hole in the middle—and it's not very tall—only ten floors. And there is a swimming pool in the middle of the hole—very deep—no children allowed. And water overflows the glass walls of the Glazed Donut and the sides of the pool, giving the impression of a sugar glaze. And all the rooms have windows overlooking the pool so everyone can see the swimmers—the hairy legs of men—and the hairless legs of women—but not their faces—unless they are diving into the water. It's quite a marvel to watch—the 77th wonder of the world. Honeymooners hold hands and jump into the hole of the Glazed Donut from the top floor—and from every room guests can point and laugh at the naked couples falling through the air—with their privates dangling: *look at that one—it'll freeze to death!* Because the pool is freezing. It's made to simulate the icy waters of Siberia. Everyone wants what he doesn't have—and since Puerto Rican waters are usually warm—Hotel El Exterminator offers the icy thrill of Siberian waters—and to feel strong like a Russian bear—and to scream shrill like an American in a horror movie—or on a roller-coaster—any sensation other than the cozy, lukewarm temperature of Puerto Rican waters—because frogs and Puerto Ricans die of coziness when they feel so, so comfortable in lukewarm waters. And this new sensation of icy cold incited someone to shout: *hey, let's open all the windows and swim in our rooms!* Everyone loved the idea—what a thrill—to open all the windows, flood the rooms with icy waters, and swim around the Glazed Donut. It was quite a sight to behold. A horror movie. Everyone was drowning in the freezing waters and looking for a fire extinguisher instead of a fire exit to escape Hotel El Exterminador, which was exterminating all of them with the icy flood of Siberian waters. But once a tourist opened a door to the

earth—they all poured out of that door like pennies and penuries
out of a piggybank—and they landed in the sand—felt the warmth of
the sea, the sun, the suntan, and the clouds.

[Giannina, on top of a tree in El Escambrón, overlooking the white dome of El Capitolio on the horizon.]

Cockroach: The allies are here—England, Germany, and Spain—with their *armadas invencibles*. They are not here to defend Puerto Rico, but to reclaim their characters—Hamlet, Zarathustra, and Segismundo.

Giannina: Tell them to come talk to me. Have the reptiles left yet?

Cockroach: Yes, they left.

Giannina: Bring England, Germany, and Spain.

England: We came looking for Hamlet.

Giannina: Actually, he is already inside me.

Germany: Where is Zarathustra?

Giannina: You will never find him unless you create him first.

Spain: And Segismundo?

Giannina: I had him as my first communion—as my host. You know what I mean, I ate him. He is already a part of me.

England, Germany, and Spain: So, we are part of you.

Giannina: You are already part of me.

Germany: We heard Zarathustra is in danger. There is war. Where is he?

Giannina: Some people you will never discover unless you create them first. He was made to be learned by heart—to be memorized, to be legendized—not to be read. He told me he was better eaten. So I ate him. Now you will not find him unless you eat me first. First read me, and then you will find the him that is in me—the Germany that has become a little island in the Caribbean—the smallest of the Antillas Mayores. I don't know if I forced myself on him—or if he willingly followed me in my meanderings through New York City, Liberty Island, and the Isle of the Blessed. But I can tell you one thing—I had dread in my eyes—and he cured me. He closed my eyes and touched my eye lids with his fingertips—and massaged them up and down—and while he massaged them—I was envisioning a different world—I was walking miles and miles ahead of my time—there were two roads—one meeting the other—and greeting it also—shaking the hand of the other—if roads instead of crossing each other were capable of shaking hands—like shaking their destinies—like inviting one another to step into each other's territory—like meeting each other halfway—but never halfway—because both of us—Zarathustra and I—were giving our best and recognizing in each other a part that we hadn't given to one another—an understanding that we never knew we understood—until our roads crossed and shook hands with each other—a joyful recognition of life—a life we never lived—until we started living with each other.

Spain: Where is Segismundo?

Giannina: He is the prince of Poland.

Spain: Return him to Spain where he belongs.

England: No, I won't return the Elgin Marbles to Greece so you can keep Hamlet.

Giannina: In Denmark?

England: In New York.

Cockroach:	♫ *La cucaracha, la cucaracha,* *Ahora puede caminar,* *Porque ya tiene,* *Porque ya anda,* *con cuatro patas para andar.*
Reptile:	Where are the cockroaches? It's not easy to crawl in the sand dunes of el Hotel El Exterminador. Let Oliver, Captain Oliver Exterminator extinguish them with his raid of fumigation. They are singing happily from every corner of the four poles: north, east, west, south. Bring the raid, the spray. Fumigate.
Oliver:	Who called me?
Reptile:	We need your song as an inspiration.
Oliver:	♫ *Oliver Exterminator* *Entonando esta canción* *Oliver Exterminator* *Es por siempre el campeón.*
Reptile:	(*moving his tail while Oliver sings his jingle*)
Cockroach:	♫ *La cucaracha, la cucaracha,* *Ahora puede caminar,* *Porque ya tiene,* *Porque ya anda,* *con cuatro patas para andar.*

Reptile: They're all deserting us. What's happening? They're uniting with the cockroaches.

Oliver: They were never reptiles to begin with. They were Dominicans, Cubans, Puerto Ricans, Mexicans, Panameños, Hondureños, Guatemaltecos, Chiletinos, Argentinos…

[At El Morro.]

G.I.: Failures in intelligence. Crack the code of Parmenides. Open the nut of Zeno. Where's Giannina?

G.I.: She is the one we can't find. She disappeared. Some say in Mayaguez. Others in Ponce.

Reptile: She is hiding en el Escambrón. A reptile disguised as a cockroach spotted her talking to Socrates.

Oliver: Socrates is en el Hotel San Juan. Check the bar 'n grill.

Reptile: I'm only reporting to you what was reported to me: she's hiding en el Escambrón.

Segismundo: Where is Hamlet? I wonder if he betrayed us and went to fight for the reptiles.

Giannina: No, I sent him to el Hotel San Juan.

Segismundo: For what?

Giannina: To study with Socrates how to become a good man.

Socrates *(sitting on a cloud):* This is the cloud that Aristophanes said I am always on.

Hamlet: Cloud 9. You have to get to cloud 10.

Socrates: Don't forget what we are here for. You were taken away from progress when you were young. When your father died you were brought back to Denmark from Wittenberg. In Wittenberg I was seeing real progress in your soul—real progress—through the meanders of your soul. We were walking—you and I—with questions and answers. I was telling you:

> *There is a higher standard of expectation.*
> *There is a higher standard of living.*

You were saying you could not afford a higher standard of living. That is what Anglo-Saxons always say—we can't afford it. They value what they can't afford more than what they can afford. No, they can't afford a lesson on how to become a good man, but they can afford to file a lawsuit. The progress I am talking about has nothing to do with getting a promotion—or being able to afford a cleaning lady—or treating a friend to dinner. The logic of affordability is stopping progress here. Do I give up on you, Hamlet?

Hamlet: Please, don't. How can I learn to be happy in adversarial times? Happiness, Socrates, comes

258

with freedom—and freedom with material wealth.

Socrates: You are forfeiting your creative daemon, and it will avenge you. I guarantee you that.

Hamlet: That happened, Socrates, that happened. Now I want to live a happy life. Giannina sent me to el Hotel San Juan to study with you how to become a happy man.

Socrates: I have to consult my creative daemon. I am not allowed to take you as a disciple unless Theaetetus and Charmides agree with Diotima—that I should give you a second chance—a second wing—to fly, birdy, fly. I don't know if you have ability for philosophy, for abstract thought. Just for saying—to be or not to be—that is the question. No, Hamlet, that is not the question. There is no question between the two—nor is there a drama or a dilemma or a tragic spot in Achilles' heel. Life encompasses life—the driving forces conjoin and enrapt them—not separation of forms and genres and genders—they are together as one—and tears seven times salt come as a comedy of errors—and a tragedian is also a comedian—and life is not black on one side and white on the other—nor is to be or not to be the question—please, no, no longer. The separation between life and death—as if it were like that, no. To be is not to be and not to be is to be—to be is definitely not to be—and life is here—being—what you, Hamlet, killed with your self-loathing—exactly that—the being alive—the potency and creativity of feeling good, healthy, wealthy, and alive.

Don't forget what that bard thought of you—player—you are *merely* a player. I'm not interested in plays—so out of tune with the being—with what is happening in this society of consumerism—so out of tune with the self—so out of fashion. What silenced poetry as our way of communicating? The newscasters who replaced the bards of ancient times only report the politics of the here and now—what browns their noses as they kiss the ass of the establishment. The bards, the prophets, and Teiresias were called upon, and Diotima also, to spell wisdom—in time again and time future—to foresee—to have visions. But newscasters stop the visions and visionaries from spilling the beans because they think the spilling of beans brings bad luck—because the visions can't be controlled—and the newscasters want to control the spilling of the beans from high heaven—so they block the spilling of the beans—why? We don't miss bad luck. Who misses bad luck? Nobody. But Diotima of Mantineia stopped the plague from entering the city for more than ten years, which is three more than what the Bible calls seven years of fat cows (good luck) and seven years of thin cows (bad luck). She stopped bad luck from entering the city for more than ten years. That's good luck—and it came with a visionary—a wisdom seeker—a seer—a prophet—a midwife—a philosopher—my teacher of love.

To see what was and what still is—what was and what still is—is life as a consequence of life—anything that interrupts this consequence from giving birth to more birthing—anything that interrupts the continuity with a selfish purpose—the newscasters always announcing the accidental—the verb coming without a noun and a predicate—the news without visions—the present without an integration into the past and the future—forecast by the relationship we have with the past—with what has happened that is bound to happen again—not as a repetition of historical events—but as knowledge of what is yet to come with the everlasting experience of the wheel of fortune of three tenses bouncing the ball on a tennis court—and I am not merely playing—I am counting my days—the ones I didn't play on the court of clowns and buffoons as my days—happy days are here again!

[Zeno, eating a melon. Parmenides, eating ice cream.]

Socrates: It is superfluous.

Parmenides: What is superfluous?

Socrates: Whipped cream on top of ice cream. If you were really hungry—hungry for thoughts—you wouldn't be eating whip cream on top of your ice cream. You must be really hot. The ice is melting.

Parmenides: I have a light cold—a slight fever—no story to tell—a bone to pick—and you, of all people, know how degrading is logic—when you start counting numbers—and they don't add up. I told you: ask Protagoras—he is there—at the Caribe Hilton eating a grilled cheese sandwich and tomato soup—and counting the waves— as possible encounters with himself and with others. And looking for an escape from the island—surrounded by water on all sides.

Protagoras: If you study with me, your life will improve.

Giannina: It's true, my life gets better when I study with all of you sages of ancient and present times, but once I start quoting you—people throw coconuts at my head. Look, Socrates, this is what I wanted to ask you: should I change—if my life is not happy—but comfortable—should I take the chance of eliminating the comfort—in order to get the love I need to grow as an artist. I want to grow—and I have grown enormously reading all of you—but I lack a candle—I lack a pyre— a mire—a bonfire. Revolutions come with cake à la mode. There is always an insurmountable amount of energy wasted—in order to combat negativity. Positive—I want to be positive. I have to confront extermination.

Oliver: I am the exterminator of cockroaches. But I will be the exterminator of reptiles. Of poets, philosophers, lovers. I wage war against terrorism, against drugs, against nations, against people, against whatever is against. I am nothing without waging war against. What am I without waging war against…against…against. … I am the divider. I am the decider. I decide which countries have rights.

Giannina: I am ready to confront you—Oliver Exterminator. You tried to strangle me with a scarf—evil motherfucker—knowing that the only thing that I have left is my voice—and the more you tried to strangle me mute with a scarf—in the street—the louder I began to sing:

> ♫ *La cucaracha, la cucaracha,*
> *Ya no la pueden exterminar*
> *Ni los gusanos*
> *Ni los reptiles*

Ni las opciones
Ni los mandatos
Pueden matar su libertad!

There was a time when I said—let me play the game, let me select one of the options that he has given me—and I even thought—what generosity of spirit! Look, he has given me not two, but three options: Wishy, Wishy-Washy, and Washy. But the more I gave you thanks, the poorer in spirit I became—even more constrained—more denied and deprived—less of a human being—until I realized—no, these options are not real. If they were real I would feel right and I feel wrong. Like somebody—a country—is pulling my leg—by giving us options—when what we need are rights—unalienable rights—the same unalienable rights that they have. Why do I feel incompetent to make a choice—a good choice? A brilliant choice. Look, I really want to make the best choice of all: mashed, fried, or baked. Other countries have no potatoes at all, but I have the liberty to pick among three options that taste the same—but nevertheless are three—not unalienable rights—only options. My voice will extinguish your extermination. I don't need your spray of raid of sex and race. Just my voice. And my voice was driven out of my neck, it was driven out of my throat, it is walking and singing alone without a neck, without a throat, without a body—my voice was driven out of my body by your strangulation—and it took my breath away—and as I stopped breathing—my voice became the voice of the people—and it started singing ferociously—fearlessly—and it started out as a shy contralto—and it became a fearless soprano—singing—fearlessly. Nobody, *ecoutez moi*—nobody is going to silence my voice— not even death will shut my mouth—not even Oliver's strangulation will stop me from saying what I have to say—what I have to say will be said and is said—with this voice—that keeps singing after the strangulation—more adamant—more passionate—like the swan song when it knows it's about to die—but also like the reptile's tail that continues moving—even after it has been dismembered from the body—it jumps to high heaven—gymnastic tails that have no origin and no end—except in the jumping away—and singing without lungs or a throat—in a scream disproportionate—disembodied—the voice left the body and sings without a body:

> ♫ *La cucaracha, la cucaracha,*
> *Ya no la pueden exterminar,*
> *Ni los gusanos,*
> *Ni los reptiles,*
> *Pueden matar su libertad!*

[Giannina, swarmed by cheering cockroaches, climbs aboard La Armada Invencible to welcome the fleet.]

Giannina: Without China I would not be able to do this. I owe it to the Chinese like you, Fidel, owe it to the Russians.

Fidel: But you managed extremely well, throwing those cocos. The Spanish fleet brought me here. On its way to Puerto Rico, La Armada Invencible stopped by Cuba and picked me up. They said: bring the children and the old men and women. I am an old man myself—so I came aboard.

Giannina: I always admired you—and Hugo Chávez too. Grab a mop—Obama said—don't criticize my grip—at least I am mopping the floor. And I say to Obama—why are you mopping the floor—public servant—when you should be leading the country. Look up—you won't have to mop the floor—if you look up and see there is a leak in the ceiling. You will never stop mopping the floor—public servant—unless you start looking at the causes—not at the consequences. The leader of a country should not be mopping the floor—nor finding leaks in the ceiling either—nor calling upon the citizens to do more for the country by mopping the floor. I will not mop the floor—nor will I look for leaks in the ceiling. I will create a country that you will not discover unless you read me first.

Cockroach:	The masses are fearless in the streets.
Giannina:	What are they doing?
Cockroach:	Screaming.
Giannina:	That's good.
Cockroach:	But they're not in your favor.
Giannina:	Even better.
Cockroach:	They're in favor of themselves.
Giannina:	Even better. The coming insurrection.
Cockroach:	The problem is Oliver Exterminator.
Giannina:	Exterminator exterminates insurrections with a spray of raid.
Cockroach:	Instigator, you're the instigator of the coming insurrection. They will blame you.
Giannina:	I won't defend myself. I am an insurrection. Good that they are defending themselves. The power should not be in the halo of one body, but in the body of the masses.
Cockroach:	Hey, who called *les Chinois*?

Segismundo: The reptiles violated the trilateral agreement we signed in the crown: Puerto Rico gets independence—the U. S. of B. pesos—and *les Chinois* power. But the U. S. of B. spent it right away in Afghanistan, in Iraq, in Iran. They were so deep in debt—almost bankrupt— naked lunch bankrupt—that they decided to attack Puerto Rico. They thought China would stop the war with money. By paying all their debts. But the breach of contract made Hu and How angry. They said:

—No more money! Now it's war!

But Americans don't go to war against their equals—unless they have allies—and this time they have no allies—not even the Georgians are getting involved because they feel Puerto Rican in relation to Russia. So the reptiles are running away—cowards. They don't want to battle the red dragon—plus the Spanish fleet La Armada Invencible—plus Fidel—plus Chávez—plus Morales—plus Lula—plus Kirchner—plus Sarkozy—Medvedev and Putin who are all on Puerto Rico's side. And the people, what are they doing?

Cockroach: They don't know what to do.

Giannina: We will win this war. The stars are on our side— aligned in favor of liberty. Who would have thought that liberty was so important—when you don't have it—but I always was free. I always said what I feel. Some people were offended because my liberty intimidated them—it made them feel that they were not free. I wanted them to feel that breach between what they didn't have and what they should have—but some of them saw that breach—and instead of swimming to the other side—to what they should have—they stayed in what they didn't have—and then they opposed what they should have had—because they had to make an effort—and the effort was too big.

Cockroach:	Look, they are coming toward us—imploring, on their knees.
U. S. of B.:	I never meant to hurt you. Please, forgive me, Puerto Rico. My house was in foreclosure. My credit cards were blocked. My unemployment benefits ran out. And I had no health insurance. All I wanted was more money from China.
Giannina:	You know what el Che says. When you are *un guerrillero*—and that's what I am—sometimes you have to play dead—for years—so that they think you are dead—and you can work on your liberation. When you decide to be free—after depending for a long, long time—and you say—I can't stand it anymore!—it's because many times before you said—I can't stand it anymore!—and you kept standing it longer than you should have because even though you couldn't stand it anymore—you were afraid that with change all hell would break loose—but when you said for the last time—I can't stand it anymore!—your patience had reached the point where it was the last straw that broke the camel's back—and all hell broke loose. I can write about many things and disguise my desires through many appetites that I satisfy in order not to confront the reality of a nation that has been misused and mistreated—undervalued—underpaid—denied—deprived. I keep hope alive with my torch of happiness inside—and my two flags

on the tip of my tongue—speaking in Spanish, Spanglish, and English—but I can't delete from the computer of my mind my unalienable right—liberty—that has been denied by more than a hundred years of American colonization. And to transform an unalienable right of a nation to be free into an if—if you vote to be free, or if you vote to be a state, or if you vote for the status quo. Don't give false options—make an unalienable right an unalienable right—don't make it an option—because you know it's not an if. I can no longer deny that I am not free—and that my country is not free—and that the voting system has cancelled the right to be a right—and has reduced it to a clause—a presupposition—a condition—if. If is not the issue—and liberty is not an issue—nor a ballot box—but a right. But like the psychics in the streets always say to me:

>—*You have a smile on your face, but deep inside you are not happy.*

You don't have to go so far as deep inside. From the outside you know I am not happy—because I am denied the three unalienable rights: life, liberty, and the pursuit of happiness.

Cockroach:	They say your declaration is treason.
Giannina:	It came from the heart. It's what every heart wants— to be free. But then we have second thoughts:

> *—How will we survive? Look at Haiti. Look at Cuba.*

Those are cucos they put in our heads. But we overcame those cucos and threw cocos instead. To crack skulls—to see what is inside their brains.

Cockroach:	Prepare for the coming insurrection. Gusanos are everywhere in San Juan, in Miami, in New York. Everywhere.
Giannina:	You always have to deal with betrayal—those who want to live on welfare—who want others to define them—who keep saying that what is little is big and what is big is little. They don't believe in themselves—that's the real problem. They don't believe they can make it—so they don't want you to make it—especially if they knew you when you were little. They think if they knew you back then, they know you now, and you're not allowed to change.
Cockroach:	Maybe they don't want what you want. They're happy being who they are—tourists in their own land. And they want to continue being

conquistadores who marry exterminators. They don't want to lose what little power they have—undeserved—because they don't earn it—they inherit that power to be the rulers of a colony in shambles—in ruins. So they continue sucking the milk of the holy cow without questioning their masters. They're very loyal to the masters—and their loyalty is rewarded with the power to maintain the status quo—the devil they know.

Giannina: It was a declaration of love for the Puerto Rican people, by the Puerto Rican people, of the Puerto Rican people. They recognize that I'm saying what they've been feeling without words for a very long time. Who among us has not been colonized by a colonizer? We all have to decolonize ourselves. To become free. Then we can begin to think about the unification of the North and the South—the Americas—but first everybody has to dance to the rhythm of his own drum:

♫ *I want to live in America!*

There is a large population within America that is still not part of America because they still want to be where they have not been able to be. I'm amazed how easily they took the name of two continents to name one nation—something smaller. Blessed be thy nation. But now

I'm going to take back the name of the nation and put it where it belongs. It is the name of two continents not of one nation.

♫ *I want to live in America!*

And whenever they sing it in *West Side Story*— they sing it with impatience:

♫ *I want to live in America! I can't wait for it to happen—when is it going to happen—that we all live in America!*

And their knees are shaking—and they're bent over—dancing with their knees shaking—saying:

♫ *I can't wait for it to happen! When is it going to happen! We're still waiting to live in America!*

First, three things must happen for this to happen. Respect the Declaration of Independence of the Islands of Puerto Rico, number one. Open the doors of the Republic to philosophers, poets, and lovers, number two. Three, eliminate *la leyenda negra*.

Declaration of Love

[A serenade to Diotima on the steps of the White House.]

Giannina: Diotima, are you going to continue holding onto your secrets forever? Open the doors of the Republic to poets, philosophers, lovers. Here are the keys. If Socrates gets angry when he sees you—just impart more wisdom to him the way you explained to him the meaning of love.

Diotima: Open the doors yourself. But don't let all the poets sneak in. Only the ones that know the Abracadabra:

> —*Ella estaría olvidadiza*
> *cuando él se perdiera en el bosque de*
> *sepias.*

But he would have to get lost in order to find himself. Losing oneself is essential to finding oneself. Are you willing to get lost in the forest of sepias?

Giannina: I've been lost for a long time.

Diotima:	I'm not talking about lost time. Time passes like sepias—they can't be found or replaced. When nights falls, people talk. Are you willing to get lost in the forest of sepias?
Giannina:	I got lost between languages. Dispersing my energy in code-switching. As if it were a switch, I turned off the lights of my language: Spanish. Click: Spanglish. Click: English-only now. I lost *cariño* and caresses. Where is the magic of the word love in the English language? Whom can I love who speaks English with an accent? Who will develop my line of thoughts—my capacity for abstraction? Do you know that I do what I do in spite of my family, in spite of my country, in spite of myself? I'm lost in the forest of sepias looking for wild mushrooms, looking for wild asparagus, looking for wild strawberries.
Diotima:	I was never born. I will never die. I live among the cherry blossoms. When people ask me when my birthday is, I remain silent. I was never born. I have been here since the beginning. I pass from one generation to the next. I see the ones who are born, and I help the ones who are awakening to awaken. This is my magic wand. I touch them with it and clean their messes—so there are no traces. Sometimes I tell them: leave traces so they'll know you were here. You were born. So you will die. But I was never born. So I will never die. I prefer poets

who are in love because they can create the
state of mind I am usually in. But they can only
capture the traces, the *pinceladas*—the rainbows—after the rain. They don't know what it
takes to remain—and to see the changes and to
provoke the changes—the birthing—of multiples—and to do the mathematics of affliction—
and to remain silent most of the time. To only
say the necessary words. The transitory words.
The ones that advance spiritual progress from
one generation to the other. Wisdom is in the
blinking—it is also in the pupils—dark pupils,
very dark—when the eyes are bright and open
to the sky. I can stop the rain like I stopped the
plague from entering the city of Mantineia for
more than ten years. Seasons are the birthing of
multiples. When I burp a child is born. When
I yawn, it's because I am bored—not because I
have a predisposition toward philosophy. If I
can control the weather—it's to stop bad things
from happening. I only provoke good things. I
wish I were born—so I could have a baby. But
I remain to pass the torch of awakening and
surviving. I have never struggled for anything.
People see me come and go. What must always
remain long is my hair—a sign of my longev-
ity. When you say: I am in the mood for love—
I provoked the feeling. I impart the fluency
of language—the fluency of love disparaged.
Everything has been here for centuries to come.
I take the props from backstage—put them in

the forefront of life—then I step aside—I am never in the way—but I am always writing messages in the sky with my magic wand. The signature is here—see the rainbow, it means something good is coming.

Giannina: We can meet (on equal terms) at the café outside. But we cannot meet (on equal terms) at your house as a consolation prize for me standing alone, singing:

> ♫ *Ábreme la puerta*
> *Que estoy en la calle*
> *Y dirá la gente*
> *Que esto es un desaire*

So, after more than a hundred years—you will finally open the doors—for me to enter—but it's because you feel you have dismissed me for too long—that you show consideration—invite me to the White House for coffee in the morning—and you think I will be satisfied with the invitation to have breakfast at the White House—now that you are finally opening the doors to poets, philosophers, lovers who have been following closely the news of the world: the good, the bad, the ugly.

Diotima: Don't doubt the invitation—a good will invitation. Take it at face value.

Giannina: I want to be invited (on equal terms) as a citizen of the world—as a Puerto Rican—with my own embassy (to stand alone) next to the White House—not as a consolation prize—for having been dismissed, denied, and deprived—not Diotima—not because you feel a little guilty.

Diotima: Why would I feel guilty?

Giannina: Because I discovered who you are.

Diotima: Who am I?

Giannina: The Statue of Liberty. Now you invite me to the White House because you know you have invited so many nations—and you never invited me (on equal terms) even though I was part of your nation. And you know it, I really, really loved you.

Diotima: The truth is I feel loved by you—but I don't want your love—in a way it is an abuse—unrequited love.

Giannina: Invite me at night when the real head honchos, the big bully countries enter the doors of the Republic. Invite me to a black-tie dinner, not to a basket of muffins as a consolation prize.

Diotima: Any poet would jump at the offer.

Giannina:	I am not any poet.
Diotima:	The doors, as you well know, are only half open. I am looking through the doors outside—and I tell you: come on in for breakfast. The secretary of state of the Republic of Uganda has just left. You have a chance to speak now. And you are rejecting the offer.
Giannina:	No, I'm saying (on equal terms) come outside. Let's both go out of our way.
Diotima:	Well, you know, I hardly know you. You are a foreigner.
Giannina:	How many foreigners have eaten breakfast at your house—and have been invited back for cocktails—only to turn you into a beggar—begging them not to leave you in disarray, in terror of yourself?
Diotima:	I can't just open my doors to every beggar, terrorist, or poet who comes knocking. I opened this time halfway (Wishy-Washy) because of the way you knocked—it had humor—it had style. I had to say—now, that's a rhythmic sassy rap. So, accept the invitation.
Giannina:	(On equal terms.) Diotima, come out to see the sun. You've been down in the cave for centuries. Even Socrates told you—Diotima, come

out of the cave into the limelight where poets, philosophers, lovers have breakfast, lunch, and dinner.

Diotima:

I don't want to go out—I want you to come on in.

Giannina:

Outside is better. It's a beautiful day. I can defend myself better (on equal terms). Diotima, this will be the final call. Is Socrates there? Is that why we're not allowed? Is he still badmouthing poets, philosophers, lovers, everybody? Is it Zarathustra who is keeping you company? Your friends are miffed that you don't answer our calls. But I understand you, Diotima. I know something funny must be going on in there for you not to answer our calls. I am sorry I insulted a member of your congregation. I told him—*Go back to wherever the hell you came from!* I didn't mean it. I am sorry. Don't punish me. Please don't take away the feather you put in my cap— as the junior member of your congregation. Let me be a senior member. It's about time, don't you think? I was jealous, you know. I didn't mean to insult him. I had no idea he was the secretary of state of the Republic of Uganda. He earned you by buying you breakfast. Can I buy you lunch? I need to see you—to go on making poems about love. I'm not a mystic—I'm mundane and profane—strumming the guitar and shaking the maracas. I want to serenade you:

♫ *Ábreme la puerta*
Ábreme la puerta
Que estoy en la calle
Y dirá la gente
Que esto es un desaire

And *el desaire* was gone with the wind—what was gone with the wind was my hat. I am not a parishioner of your church. I am not an addict—nor a fanatic—I am a poet of love. And why do you need my poems of love? When you make love to Protagoras, to Aristophanes, to Parmenides, to Zeno—you ask me to write the happening—but I am not allowed in—just to peek through a window—without touching any of the bodies—as a premonition of happiness—a glimpse of what could happen—if you let me love all these sages of humanity.

Diotima: All these yawners with a predisposition for philosophy with their sneezes and hiccups and headaches—who don't act on impulses—who refrain from their desires—who find themselves in a dilemma—without a beginning and an end—I am here to heal them—by sleeping with them—they become healthy in a second—they stop thinking. Their thoughts are their eternal dilemmas—what gives them headaches—and keeps them from making love to each other and to me. See what happens—when the doors of the Republic are opened to poets, philosophers, and lovers—orgies of love—and magic spells spill champagne and baby teeth start growing trees inside gums—and people laugh to high heaven—and they drink—and forget—what is mindless—the mindless mind of the mindless world—what goes around—and never returns when you want it to come to you fast—efficacy without memory. I make them forget who they think they are—for a second the mindless mind starts spitting wisdom—the best thoughts come after the mindless mind has made love to me. Making love to me turns their predisposition toward philosophy into an outright disposition—a position—a possession of the miracles that happen when you make love to Diotima—and if a baby yawns—it is not because he is destined to be a philosopher—but because he is hungry for food—hungry for sleep—hungry for love—like all these lonely people—where do they all come from?

Giannina: Let's simplify the philosophy of making love to a poet.

Diotima: What you recognize in me as your predisposition toward a philosophy of love is my way of making love to you—my way of giving babies to the world, babies of the mind, who yawn with a predisposition to life born crying—with pampers—shit—and no ideals—shitty diapers—and teething screams that don't even know they are screaming—words that don't recognize where they come from—they simply slip out of the slippers—like growth spills out of ages—and progress spills out of spirituality—when spiritual progress is not traumatic—but fluent—babies are born crying—and poets—out of fluency—when the fluency of love spills the truth of happiness—and it seems like a miracle, that all this happiness happens without a miracle, without a thought, without a predisposition to philosophy, just by the touch of a poet who looks straight into my pupils and becomes my pupil.

Giannina:

I invited you to a glass of champagne—and we drank the whole bottle. But then Laches, Charmides, and Theaetetus came over—and you pretended that you were with me—but you left with all three—and closed the doors as you left—and I heard the dynamic of the situation—and the lies were clumsy—and I gathered the utensils and cooked the *azafrán*—the champagne spilled—and I was alone—writing the traces that you were leaving everywhere—and you elected all of them into your company—and created gradations—and I graduated with a PhD in your way of electing members—and I saw in your pupils—all your pupils had very black pupils and bright violet eyes—and they were cats. Charmides had the charm of a cat—Laches, the milk of a cat—and Theaetetus could meow like a cat—but I could only bark to high heaven like a dog.

Diotima: I never gave you just one grape, Giannina. I gave you a bunch of bananas and grapes—a bunch of cherries—a bunch of strawberries—a bunch of asparagus—a bunch of bunches—and when I offered you the cherries—it's because they had the pit of poetry inside. Stop looking down for trinkets. Trinkets like pennies bring penuries. Look up to the treetops to find the fruits of *la buena cosecha*—to get the plenties. Stop frequenting the few—they rarely become plenty—in plentitude—in plenitude—frequent the plenty—in plenitude—in plentitude. Plentitude has fortitude as its frontispiece. Look always at the front of things—things have a front—and they give a front—and sometimes it's a front to hide something bad—but this frontitude is not hiding something bad—it's a sign of fortitude—it wheels ponds into rivers, into seas—inducing the birthing of multiples—and arousing the tickles of the feathers of the rainbow when the peacock opens its tail. Induce the plenties to be born—effortlessly—with tickles, sneezes, headaches, yawning, and clapping of hands. The effortless effort of letting the river run to the sea—inducing the birthing of multitudes, in plenitudes, in plentitudes. You have to learn, Giannina, some bunches of bananas don't get along with the grapes—some dogs try to meow because they think I prefer cats—and I do prefer cats—but if I see a dog like you impersonating a cat—it breaks my heart—so much adoration for me that you have to meow like a cat even though you bark like a dog—all these barks like meows—in order to soften my nails—I hardly scratch—like a cat—now I give you my paw—like a dog. So many lonely people—where do they all come from? That's why they talk to cats and dogs—and go astray like cats and dogs—and relate to their neighbors through their cats and dogs—and their babies too. Because they are innocent. Innocence is what is valued—the poetry that can emerge from surface talk that is not about money or corruption but about cats and dogs on leashes and babies in carriages—and their chitchat carries their thoughts away from their daily worries where they are stranded in the mud—hardly able to move their legs of lead through the mud. I'll give myself to you, after you create me—create me first, then you can discover me.

Giannina: First tell me how you are.

Diotima: I am inclusive—I don't exclude possibilities. I have Socrates. I have you. I have Charmides, Laches, Theaetetus.

Giannina: I totally agree. We have to include—not exclude. Like Socrates—he loved Alcibiades—but he was there with Agathon when Alcibiades stormed into the party—and the three shared the bananas and grapes. Though there was a flare of jealousy in Alcibiades—it was melted down by wisdom. Jealousy doesn't exist where wisdom rules—and if you can have many— why limit yourself to one? Who says I can't love the multitudes, the multiples—and who says they can't enrich my life? Of pleasures, I take more. Of pains, less. But when wisdom rules, pain is less and less. Because wisdom includes the plenitudes, plentitudes. When there is husband and wife (only two), they want three—and three wants four—and four wants five and six. More is more. Children bring children. Multitudes bring multiples. And to be wise is to allow all the possibilities to exist—and to exist in all the possibilities that you can imagine—and then you create those imaginations—and after you create them you watch them exist in reality. I give birth to the multitudes. Let society raise the possibilities of my creations.

Diotima: You never know, society might abort them.

Giannina: They are so full of fear. Fear of the multiples— when they start multiplying their possibilities— they don't know what to do. It's morality, religion denying existence the possibility of being creative.

Eradication of Envy: Gratitude

[In Central Park, watching a squirrel eating an acorn on top of a tree.]

Hasib:

Didn't Iris Pagán tell you: don't waste your time with beginners. Well, I tell you: climb up that tree. Now, let them look up and say: that's where I dream to be. Keep a distance. Be like a squirrel—*escurridiza*—run away from them—let them dream about you—but don't allow them to lower you. They think: if she can make it, I can make it too. But they don't know what it takes. Look at that madman laughing and cursing at the same time. He wasted too much time before—now he is enjoying himself.

Giannina:

Do you know who that madman is? It's Zarathustra. One of the sages of humanity—the greatest—in my opinion after Socrates. I agree with you—now he is enjoying himself—but not because he wasted too much time—the opposite—he hardly had time to enjoy himself. He burned himself out.

Hasib:

One way or another, he burned himself out. Do you mind if I smoke a cigar?

Giannina: Go ahead. Wisdom is burned like experience exhumed—like calories are burned—through the exercise of life. It's true, now he is in the here and now, enjoying the moment. Before he was in the work—in the development of his thoughts—and burned all the calories of his thoughts—until he burned out his brain. I am so happy to have met you—you have enriched my life—exhuming wisdom—as if it were the exhumation of bones.

Hasib: We met on the road. I was driving my cab. And I told you: don't throw pearls before swine.

Giannina: But I am so accustomed to an audience of buffalos and cows. This is the kind of audience that you get in New York.

Hasib: Worse—because buffalos and cows don't say: *If she can do it, I can do it too!*

Giannina: I raise the case against *I can do it too!*—when you can't do it too.

Hasib: That's why it's best to climb the tree—and wait on top of the tree until the bad poets pass by—without confronting them—eating nuts on treetops—with your two little hands—and squirreling around the branches—getting away from them without confronting them.

Giannina: I rest my case. It is harder to recognize a poet than other artists. If a peacock spreads its tail—the buffalos and cows can't see the difference between the peacock's tail that fans the sky with its rainbow—and the cow's tail that swats flies—and the buffalos looks deep—but understand nothing.

Hasib: What do these animals have in common?

Giannina: They belong to the rabble—the multitude of bananas and grapes. But, you know what, I can't think this way. I tried—after walking with Zarathustra for such a long time—but I can't think this way.

Hasib: You identify with them.

Giannina: True, I identify with the common feelings of the multitude. That's why I write in a common language—with common feelings—and common animals—and yet—I know I am on top of that tree—and that neither the cows nor buffalos can catch me. And why would I want the common denominator? Because poetry is made of the common denominators—of oranges, bananas, and grapes. I want to connect with these common denominators and create a quality, a distinction—while all the dogs are howling. When I was a little girl, my grandmother sent me to the beauty

salon across the street from her house—and
while I was getting my hair washed—an old
woman who was seated in front of the looking
glass went deep into a trance—and started talking to spirits in tongues. I was so scared I ran out
of the beauty salon with shampoo in my hair—
all sopping and sudsy. And I think that's the
moment I became a medium of thoughts. That
old woman who was looking inside the looking
glass—when she went into a trance—transmit-
ted to me the numbness of the trance. And I
also went into the looking glass of the pupils of
Diotima. I entered the dimension of mediums—
the ones who are between fire and wind—the
ones who mix copper and smith—the ones who
wear hats to protect the fluidity of things. They
gave me two chambers—the pupils of Diotima—
they told me look inside and don't blink an eye—
as if to blink an eye were a sign of looking for an
excuse to get out—because sometimes you start
wondering—what am I doing here? They never
asked me what I do for a living—so I never asked
them what they do for a living—because they
were never born—so they would never die—
and they didn't have to earn a beginning and an
end. I was happy to lose track of my biology—to
lose track of my age—to understand suffering as
a biological constitution—and not as part of a
physical body that is aging—and is dated. I was
learning to live without an age—aging in wisdom—going forward in time. I knew I was doing

something for a living—but I didn't know what I was doing—I was just living—I had entered the chambers of the pupils of Diotima. I felt as if I were inside a lightbulb—there was so much appreciation inside that lightbulb—that even though people outside might think I was stuck—I never felt I wanted to get out of the luminosity of those pupils—even though electricity was running through my body.

Hasib: And what did you get from Socrates?

Giannina: I didn't get knowledge—but opinions—and at the end I realized that even my opinions were all wrong. I got a vessel—and a trip—and I felt good. I understood that I had to follow my creative daemon—that I could not walk alone anymore. I have grown with Socrates. I see him when Parmenides is old and Zeno is middle aged—and Socrates is young and insolent, trying to refute Parmenides—and telling Zeno that his book is Parmenides's theory upside down. I see him also talking to Protagoras—trying to pull his leg—to make a name for himself—to acquire wisdom—but also to show off that he knows more than Protagoras. And I see him later in life—I don't know how old—but definitely older—becoming a midwife to Theaetetus who has bulging eyes like Socrates himself—also ugly—and I hear in the Republic that a young boy with a predisposition toward philosophy is a boy who feels drawn back—and his characteristic is that he yawns. The fact that he yawns because he is detached, or distanced, or abstracted from himself and others draws me back to the hiccups of Aristophanes and the headache of Charmides, which is cured by a leaf and a charm that is the incantation of a poem— the incantation of the charm of words said at the same time that a leaf is passed over the forehead to alleviate the headache. Socrates learns to be a midwife from his own midwife, Diotima of Mantineia. He says that if you follow him you will gain spiritual progress. You see how your life can improve through the progress of your thoughts. What you see is that the thoughts start moving with hiccups, yawning, headaches, leaves, incantations, tickles, and sneezes. In the process of seeing Socrates grow old, I see the portraits of Socrates as a young man as I see the self-portraits of Rembrandt as a young man— and throughout his life—with his son Titus— with his wife Saskia—and above all the portraits of his very old age—the same way I see the portraits of Socrates—and the progression of his thoughts—and his whole persona—until his death. I am even present the moment he dies— when he drinks the hemlock—and I say to myself in his defense—he doesn't defend himself like a lawyer would have defended him— no, he defends himself as a philosopher—and he himself says that philosophers are not good when they appear in the court of law—because they are not trying to win at all costs—but to impart wisdom. The people he meets on the road—on the way to a party—the people he talks to—give him knowledge—but the knowledge is experience accumulated—and it's never there when it leaves you—and it always leaves you—so again you retire—open your frontiers—draw back—and become empty—to fill the glass with water—fresh water—again. So, it is a never-ending tale until it ends. And the end is not the one he sets for himself—but the limit is set for him—and he chooses his destiny—to stay—when he could have gone into exile—but he didn't—and he always was following the line of thought of the intuition—negating envy. He was against envy. Intuition is the positive energy that envy kills when it refuses to see the rainbow in the sky. He is a poet who doesn't want to open the doors of the Republic to poets—he knows himself too well—and he doesn't want to open the doors to people like himself—even though everybody opens his door for Socrates to enter his home—because when Socrates enters you know it will be an event—and who wouldn't want to be a part of his legend. And Socrates is in himself—in simplicity—always using the same words like Alcibiades said—packasses, or blacksmiths, or cobblers, or tanners—always the same—simply and intuitively—without attacking a subject matter in a negative way—when it is done in a negative way—it gets stuck—and doesn't progress. For progress to happen—spiritual progress—intuition is the driving force that is not drawn back by any bad feeling—intuition renews itself—not knowing the whereabouts of progress nor questioning the origin of progress—letting it be as it is in its simplicity—he stays there—rocking his thoughts—and never letting them get old—because they are never guilty of anything—they never have to hide—or do shameless things—everything is in the open—and when you come out of the cave—it is always progress—when the obscurity is brought to tears of shame—left behind—because spiritual progress depends on escalating degrees of light—of running into the light—of shining with the light inside—of reflecting back what has shined—and dawning—giving birth to puppies of light. They say Protagoras had a spellbinding voice—and that was half the attraction—the other half was his mesmerizing thoughts. I love when Socrates and Hippocrates go to visit Protagoras—and they knock on the door—Socrates and Hippocrates knock, knock, knock—and a eunuch opens the door—and exclaims with disdain: Sophists!—and shuts the door—right on their noses. It's as if the eunuch were taking revenge against Socrates for the harm he did to Homer—and to me—and to all the poets through the ages—because he invented that we are descriptive—distanced from creation because we represent—imitate—and we don't rise to the level of knowledge—we stay in the cave with manacles and fetters—looking at shadow puppets on the wall—but those shadows are not real—they are opinions, feelings—equivocal impressions that don't rise to the level of wisdom—and this prejudice has subsisted for centuries against poets—like the black legend that the British invented about the Spaniards that has harmed for centuries the reputation of Latins. Against these two prejudices that are shadow puppets on the wall—I have had to struggle in this society. What is it that philosophers envy about poets? Definitely not our thoughts because they say we have no thoughts and we don't create schools of followers like they do. So it is not respect they envy because they instill reverence and admiration and veneration. I think what they envy is that we are capable of love—that we have the power inside us—that we don't have to analyze that power in order to seize it—that we are the makers of the happening that happens—and that we get the credit for making it happen—without understanding the happening. But we do understand the happening. We just don't care to be recognized as the authors, the authorities, the shaman. We are voices, indistinguishable (distinguishable). You can distinguish our tones, our humors, our hiccups, our sneezes—and it is not our knowledge—but our wisdom that whistles. I am trying to get to the beginning of envy. I want to eradicate that envy that has harmed our sovereignty as poets—the disregard of intuition—the neglect—trying to make of that first intuition something that is irrelevant. I think it's more relevant than their envy. Envy is opaque. It is the negation of sight—it doesn't want to recognize. What recognizes is the sparkle in the eye—the *in love* of an empathetic eye—yes, the recognition of the sparkle, the flame, the love—even if it is dimming in the night—fragile—blinking—indecisive—shy—not secure—with low self-esteem—it shines—it blinks its eyes—and it affirms an inauguration—a rainbow—and a rainbow is the installation of an intuition—when an intuition is secure of itself—after it has rained and the gray sky turns violet and signs a rainbow—the signature of the triumph of an intuition that has installed an affirmation of life. I also think they envy our results that appear effortless. They would like to see us sweat through the hard labor of a system of reason that eliminates what we create, and they think we are not essential, but they are essential because they are radical thinkers even though they eradicate precisely that which is radical thinking—that intuition is the negation of envy—that when you feel somebody—because you believe in the intuition of a feeling—it's because you are incapable of feeling envy—because envy denies intuition—and a poet lives with sparkles, blinks, intuitions—and not with the eradication of intuition—thoughts spread like butter on bread—and they spread viruses and plagues—and they are contaminated—and some are contagious—and you need to keep a distance from a thought that is dangerous—because it is blinking red alert—nervous twitches of c'mon, what's going on? Information is going on—noses that sneeze are going on—false and redundant conclusions are going on—not conducive to thoughts—but to complements—and compliments—and they drag their legs and have to be carried—because they don't carry themselves with ease—they don't have the driving force—a direction—an intuition that is clueless because it has a clue and a cure and a remedy against the maladies of the spirit—the eradication of the philosopher's envy of the poet's intuition—the abrupt realization that a thinker can sneeze and blink an eye—and not set a terminology that is opaque—that doesn't want to recognize—even though it blinks—blanks—the intuition—and it doesn't fill in the blank—it runs and dives in the river—and it only sees the repetition but not the sparkles of light—blinky—blinky—blinky. And don't forget that it was Diotima who taught Socrates that love is not a God—because it is a desire—never full, always needy—an intermediary residing between heaven and earth—between plenty and necessity. And it was

Diotima who gave birth to his wisdom about begetting babies—she told him all humans want to beget—begetting is the secret of immortality—of the eternal recurrence of flesh, life, cries, babies—and that there are different ways of begetting—babies of the flesh but also babies of the brain—babies of knowledge—and that this is the highest way of begetting—lightning flashes of the brain—intuitions in rainbows—signatures of a celestial presence in the sky—signatures of poets in the sky. What I like most is the ticklish talk of the midwife—and how Socrates tells Diotima—begs her—impatiently—tell me, please—like a beggar—give me money—enlighten me—my spirit—free me of the shackles—let me see the sun—get me out of here—please—I beg you, Diotima, I don't know how—teach me. What you see is that he also is a medium—like love that is needy—because he is the son of plenty and necessity—yes, Socrates is also needy—he needs Diotima the midwife to help him give birth to the knowledge he begets—he begets lightning, inspiration, love, light—and he gets out of the cave (womb)—while he is giving birth—with the help of Diotima. He is not only the one who begets but the one who is begotten. I care most about knowledge when knowledge is a process—when you see the process of begetting—the process of giving light to the baby in the stable or on a bed of straw—where the baby is born to lay eggs that will hatch into chickens—with sound inside—the jingle-bell of the sound that knocks and knocks on the door to open—but the door shuts—and the sounds leave an impression in the brain. The important thing is the process of begetting—the begetting in itself—and how it happens—without the begotten—the begotten happens—as the begetting gets it—if it gets the process—the passage of one territory into another dimension where there is no space between the passages where the dwellers dwell—and they never realize they are dwelling inside the begetting of the begotten. If they realize they are passing by—like you lick an envelope to close the envelope—and lick the stamp to seal it with a kiss. Especially when the door shuts in front of the nose that breathes the knock and shut of the door. The presence gets closer—it misses the shutting of the door—by a hair—and the hair stands up and the nose releases a sneeze of relief. (*I sneeze.*) Yes, the knocking on the door of the Republic—knock knock knock—the eunuch shuts the door on Socrates who doesn't learn the lesson. He shuts the door for poets never to enter the academic world of scholars—minds without furniture to furnish, without dislocations to dislocate, without inscriptions to inscribe—with formulas to fill—minds that run out of gas in the middle of the road—and that muffle—minds that stick around—but never

stick—never pass the pathway of knowledge
without inscriptions to learn. I wonder how he
felt at that moment he was going to die—knowing the precise moment—and having said
goodbye to his disciples—to his wife—to his
children—how he decided to stay and drink the
hemlock—instead of going into exile in another
land—he decided against being a foreigner—
even though he was a foreigner in his own land.
I also wonder—how it must have felt to know
the moment—to accept it—to say goodbye after
knowing—and to die. Only a control freak—
only someone with a big ego—only someone
who knows—even the moment of his death—
and his resignation upon death. Probably he
was seeing the rainbow—the pastel colors after
the rain—how his friends would cry—and he
would express himself in the colors of the rainbow—as signatures in the sky of permanence—
as a smile in the sky—after death—as the Milk-
maid of Bordeaux after the black paintings of
Goya—as the affirmation of the Yes to life—
even after the hemlock—there is the affirmation
of his legend—and the serenity whenever
Socrates appears with the rainbow of his
thoughts—with his smile of wisdom. Life is
good—even without the protagonist of my
life—even without my chatter—there is the
cock on the roof—the rainbow in the sky—and
the preceding life—the continuation—the passing of one generation to the other—there is the

destiny of a man who can also decide when to die—though not how to die—it was decided for him—and the moment—but he had control even of his last moment—as a control freak—he could kiss today goodbye—and see the tears of his disciples and his wife. I think he was accepting the knowledge of knowing—of resignation—of life as it stays in permanence—in the eternal recurrence of what repeats itself—of the awakening of the sunsets and dawns—of the lightness of living in the intuition of life—as an affirmation of the triumph of intuition against envy—as life itself when it moves along—and comes back—without regrets—with waves of light. Why defend yourself at the end—when you didn't defend yourself throughout the multiple stages—you saw the progression of yourself—your multiple beings in their multiple relations to other beings—why shut doors at the end—when all the multiple beings are there knocking on all the doors for the doors to open—to poets, philosophers, lovers. Even death has to be an open dialogue with life—it has to go on—to move along—not to enclose a body—but to open the body to the multiples and multitudes—like at the very end of *The Symposium*—when the crowd of revelers comes marching in—knocking on the door—from the beginning of *The Symposium* to the end—all those people entering the same house of wisdom and wine—all drunk on life—no doors

closed—all in different degrees of light and
life—in layers of colors and depths of soul—in
progression into the limelight—all moving—
knocking —and entering—all talking—drinking—sleeping—dancing—and leaving—entering and leaving—the passing of energy from the
individual to the multitudes—from the multiples to the single-handed—to the elected—and
the masses of revelers—they appear as packasses, as the hemlock appears, as the Sileni
appear, as the flute girls appear, as multitudes
singled out by their birth—by their existence—
by the nature of the flock—by the birds of a
feather that flock together—by the flow of
humanity—they smell of sweat—and the repetition of the same words—always the same and
always different—in simplicity but in multiplicity—in individuality—in Socrates—but in the
packasses—in the single and the double—mark
with itself and unique in its form—and in
repeating the daily bread and the wine—the
words that keep popping up in multiplicity of
thoughts and single-handed to lend a hand and
continue passing from one hand and one ear
that hears to another pair of eyes—bulging eyes
that see—capture—question—and the pupils of
Diotima open up—like shelters in the sky—too
much is never too much—as a signature of life
from birth to hemlock—I take it as gratitude.

About the Author

Photo Copyright: Michael Somoroff

Giannina Braschi is one of Puerto Rico's most influential and versatile writers of poetry, fiction, and essays. She was a tennis champion, singer, and fashion model before she became a writer. With a PhD in the Spanish Golden Age, she has taught at Rutgers, Colgate, and City University and has written on Cervantes, Garcilaso, Lorca, Machado, Vallejo, and Bécquer. Author of the postmodern poetry classic *Empire of Dreams* and Spanglish tour de force *Yo-Yo Boing!*, Braschi's cutting-edge work has been honored by the National Endowment for the Arts, the NY Foundation for the Arts, *El Diario*, PEN, the Ford Foundation, the Reed Foundation, the Danforth Scholarship, and Instituto de Cultura Puertorriqueña. She writes in three languages—Spanish, Spanglish, and English—to express the enculturation process of millions of Hispanic immigrants in the U.S.—and to explore the three political options of Puerto Rico—nation, colony, or state. Braschi dedicates her life's work to inspiring personal and political liberation.